Caitlin's Promise

Caitlin's Promise

SEBASTIAN DAVISON

To my dear wife Liz, without whose assistance,
encouragement and unfailing support,
this book would never have seen the light of day.

CONTENTS

INTRODUCTION

The idea for this story came to me as I was walking alone in Glen Ceitlein, a little side valley leading from the beautiful larger glen of Glen Etive in Western Scotland. I had walked most of the three miles of its length and had reached a point where two streams meet as they tumble down from the higher peaks at the end of the glen.

My legs decided that it was time for me to retrace my steps but before I obeyed them I sat down on a large granite boulder to enjoy the efforts of my labours and to rest. There was little breeze and though it was cloudy it was warm. I was alone. As I munched my sandwiches and gazed at the most beautiful and tranquil scene, my mind wandered contentedly where it would, over anything, everything and nothing, I thought I heard a woman's voice. I looked round but there was nobody to be seen. It was not the voice of a person in distress, rather just a conversational tone that might be used in day to day chatter. The voice seemed to come from the burn, the little stream, where several silver birch trees were clinging precariously to the rocky bank. At any minute I expected to see someone appear from that direction but nobody appeared, that was all I ever heard. I walked over to the burn but it was deserted. I had the whole glen to myself.

Dismissing the entire episode as a figment of my imagination I packed up the remains of my lunch, filled my water bottle from the ice-cold, gurgling stream and set off back down the way I had come. When I returned to my campsite I thought little more about the episode until, as I settled down in my tiny, cosy tent for the night, tired but content, my mind began to wander back over the events of the day and although I'm not really a great believer in the supernatural or 'voices from the past', what I had experienced earlier on that day seemed to me to warrant further investigation, so I determined to look deeper into the history of Glen Ceitlein.

Over the course of the next few months I spent many interesting and occasionally frustrating hours and days researching the history, culture and folklore of this undistinguished but incredibly beautiful piece of the Highlands. I searched the internet and read as many books as I could find; I delved into local records and asked questions of as many people as I could.

In the telling of this story I have used undeniable facts of history, folklore, legend, logical conjecture, vivid imagination and pure fantasy. Make of it what you will. Perhaps you should not judge it, in part or as a whole; just enjoy the telling of a long-forgotten tale.

Seb Davison

CHAPTER ONE

It was drizzling and she was barefoot; but she didn't care. In fact she didn't even notice. Only in the coldest of the winter when a deep blanket of snow was covering the mountainside making the steep slopes slippery did Caitlin wear anything on her feet. She was too pre-occupied with her search. Her favourite cow had gone missing from the little field beside the house. Her father said the animal had escaped because it was time for her to give birth to her calf so would have managed to find a tiny hole in the fence and gone to some quiet place up on the hillside where there was plenty of shelter and protection. It was late summer and the bracken was turning to yellow, to orange and to brown making the animal's rough, pale brown coat almost impossible to spot from any distance.

Caitlin climbed higher and higher, past the bracken, on through a large patch of scrubby rowan and birch trees and up on to the clear side of the mountain. Little grew at this altitude except tussocks of short grass and the occasional stunted willow, pushed almost horizontal by the continuous winds.

By now the bottom of the glen from which she had come was obscured by a shoulder of the mountain. She was heading for an enormous outcrop of granite that jutted from the mountainside high above the little gathering of houses below. If she climbed to the top of this great rock she would be able to see the whole of the hillside and from this vantage point she hoped she would be able to discover where the calf was being born.

The path she was following took her behind the huge boulder, larger than any house, which had broken away from the towering crag above her at some time in ages past. She scrambled up the only side that was not too steep to ascend, her bare toes helping her to find the smallest foothold and on reaching the top she looked down across the hillside that she had just climbed.

Had she thought about it, Caitlin could have expected to see a quiet rural scene stretched out below her; the thin wisps of smoke, rising from the peat fires of each of the three houses, several long-haired Highland cattle grazing in the stone walled field adjoining the buildings and perhaps a few people going about their daily tasks. Never in her worst nightmares could she have ever imagined the sight that presented itself to her that day as she looked down from her vantage point above the little glen.

For many generations the population of the glen had remained fairly static; a few people came and left again, some were born, others died, but the numbers had stayed about the same. At present twenty four people with ages from three months to eighty seven years lived in the three households that made up the little settlement. Today there were probably more people in the place than at any time since man had first come to these remote places in the Scottish Highlands. Large parts of the ancient Caledonian forest, especially the large trees had been cut down, mainly to be used as charcoal at the local iron smelting works; but there was still plenty for the needs of the local population, as yet.

To Caitlin observing from above there seemed to be hundreds of strangers surrounding the houses though in actual probability there were no more than fifty. The sounds of men and women shouting were carried on the breeze to where she stood. Suddenly she heard a shot rise from the glen below; followed by a blood curdling scream, a scream so awful it would haunt her for years to come, only for it to stop abruptly. The silence was more awful than the scream.

As she watched, smoke started to drift from the doorway of one of the little houses, only small puffs at first, but it rapidly increased into large billows. Flickers of flame appeared at the windows curling upwards soon igniting the thatched roof. Within the space of three or four minutes the entire house was on fire. Soon, the other two dwellings nearby were ablaze as well. Caitlin could only stand and watch in horror as all the residents, including her own family, were surrounded by the strangers and driven almost like a herd of cattle down the little path towards the exit from the glen. Her first impulse was to rush down and try to stop whatever was happening and to help her family, but the instinct of self- preservation held her back, so she crouched down behind the boulder and watched in despair until the whole sorry procession had passed round the first corner in the path and left the glen empty and desolate.

There had been rumours passed around of late about similar acts of terrible violence and destruction, but neither Caitlin, nor anybody else living in the glen had taken any notice, never dreaming that such a thing could happen in a glen as small and remote as theirs.

The strange men Caitlin could see in the glen were the henchmen and bully boys of the Duke of Sutherland and although they called themselves soldiers, they were nothing of the kind. 1799 saw the demand for wool reach an all-time high. Until the conflict between England and Napoleonic France, Flanders had supplied large quantities of wool and woollen cloth to English merchants who, without this source had been unable to keep up with demand, especially for all the military uniforms that were required. And so, now that the Flemish wool was unavailable, to take advantage of this shortage and the consequent high prices and thinking to make themselves a great deal of money, the Duke and many other owners of land in the Scottish Highlands deemed that it would be more profitable to increase the number of sheep on their estates. They simply took over most of the land that was at present occupied by the indigenous inhabitants and turned their little farms over to large-scale wool production. These landed gentry, mostly of English origin, regarded these people whom they considered to be nothing more than simple peasants, to be 'expendable' and 'unnecessary' for the new enterprises, apart from a few that would be retained as shepherds. It was proposed that they should be rehoused in areas less favourable to sheep farming where they could find 'alternative additional employment to augment their income; probably by fishing.' In reality the new locations to which they were sent were totally inadequate to sustain these dispossessed people and although some moved away or emigrated, many simply starved to death; not quickly but by slow, insidious malnutrition that made them more susceptible to other diseases like pneumonia or tuberculosis.

In actual fact, despite their condescending words and phrases, these absentee landlords couldn't have cared less about their tenants and so employed the unsavoury characters like those that had come to the girl's village to remove these 'Obstacles' by any means they found necessary. Livestock was slaughtered, houses burned. Rape and murder were commonplace.

Just as Caitlin was about to descend to the little village to do what or to find what she had no idea, she saw a figure whom she recognized as her uncle Iain running back up the path towards the burning buildings, followed at some distance by one of the 'Enforcers'. On reaching his burning house, Iain braved the smoke and the fire to start pulling stones from the outside of the end wall at the base of the chimney. His follower or pursuer, Caitlin did not know which, paused and hid behind a wall at the side of the path some distance from the house. As soon as Iain had made a hole in the stonework, he lay down, thrust his arm into the wall and withdrew a bundle about two feet long wrapped in sacking. Clutching it to his chest he turned and started to run back the way he had come. When he reached the wall behind which his pursuer was hiding, the man stepped from his place of concealment. A flash of steel, the thrust of a claymore. Iain fell and was still. Bending, the man roughly dragged the fallen man onto his back and pulled the bundle from his arms. The sacking fell away to reveal a gleam of yellow metal. Caitlin immediately recognised the object her uncle's attacker now held in his hands. It was an ornate candlestick, supposedly gold, though probably it wasn't and the most precious possession of her uncle. It was reputed to have come from a ship of the Spanish Armada that had been wrecked in a storm on the shores of the island of Mull over a hundred years before.

This beautiful ornament was only ever displayed on special occasions; Christmas, Easter and one night that she would never forget, when Caitlin was taken to her uncle's house to visit her aunt as she lay dying. The only light in the room had been from a thick beeswax candle, burning in the holder on the top of the precious candlestick. The flickering light from the soft yellow flame reflected in the golden metal gave the whole room an eerie glow. This, and the knowledge that somebody whom she had been close to all her life was soon to die had left Caitlin, at eight years old with what would be an indelible memory that she would recall many times through-out her life. Whenever she encountered the unmistakeable smell of burning beeswax, her memory would take her straight back to that little room and her first connection with the death of a loved one.

The killer gave the body a final glance, stooped, plucked a handful of grass and carefully wiped his bloody claymore before returning it to its scabbard. He tucked the candlestick into his tunic and set off back down the path to re-join his companions and the bewildered villagers on their journey into the unknown.

This then was the scene that had unfolded before Caitlin Munroe on that late September day in 1799. Just fifteen years old, at first glance, Caitlin was a fairly unremarkable girl; no different to many other Scottish lassies; beautiful, long fair hair with a touch of red, clear pale skin with a few freckles that would fade as she grew older, long legs and with a promise of robust elegance and grace, she would develop into a very beautiful woman. However there was something else, something that set her apart from other girls. She had an inner strength, and a determination to complete whatever she decided to do. But she was still very young with the innocence and naivety of someone born and brought up in remoteness and isolation. The things she had just seen had frightened her so much that she was beyond rational thought. She turned and ran. Ran towards the only place where she knew she would be safe from harm.

High up on the side of the mountain above the village, in a narrow cleft there was a small cave hidden from view by a high waterfall, not a large one in volume, but enough to mask the entrance to the cavern from inquisitive eyes. The overhanging lip of rock threw the water far enough forward to allow access from the side without being soaked. This little cave had been well known to many generations of the inhabitants of Glen Ceitlein. It was surprisingly dry and inviting considering the watery entrance. Stretching some forty feet or more back into the mountain, this secret hideaway was large enough to hold several people and was recognised as the place where the adolescents could gather away from adult interference. The climb up the steep slopes above the glen required considerable effort, only attempted in the exuberance of youth. It was possible to light a small fire undetected in a natural recess at the back of the cave, to give warmth, comfort and light, with the spray from the waterfall masking any smoke. Many a relationship had blossomed in this private place, hidden from inquisitive eyes. Caitlin had been to the cave with her friends a number of times before and instinctively knew that she would be safe in this secret place; safe from 'the soldiers' who would have no knowledge of its existence.

She made the entire climb without pausing for a rest, her muscles fuelled by the adrenalin of fear. She arrived gasping for breath and trembling from head to foot with exhaustion and a mixture of relief and terror. She crawled into the back of the cave as far from the light as possible, wrapped herself in a piece of homespun woollen cloth worn by all the people in the village and known as a plaid, that had been left there by some previous visitor and waited. Her mind was trying to make sense of all she had just observed, but for now all she could see was an incoherent world of visions; coming and going, advancing and retreating, overlapping and confusing. Knowing that she was safe, she began to relax a little and after a while, she slept.

When she awoke a few hours later, darkness had fallen and the rain had cleared away. Even though the light was very dim at the back of the cave she could see the moonlight shining through the cascade of water falling in front of the cave entrance. A truly wondrous sight, but one to which Caitlin gave no thought. She was much calmer now and although she did not really understand the full implication of the day's events, she realized that her life in the glen was over.

She suddenly remembered that there was a little wooden box on a small ledge high up on the cave wall that often contained a small quantity of food left over from previous visits. Groping in the almost total darkness she finally managed to locate it and once open, she discovered that all the box contained was several oatmeal biscuits and three small baked potatoes, shrivelled but edible. She ate the potatoes, peeling back the unappetising, blackened skin before nibbling the cold white interior, drank from the waterfall, cupping her hands to catch the water as it fell from the rock above, then crept cautiously from the cave into the moonlit night.

As Caitlin scrambled down the steep slopes of the glen she could smell the acrid smoke that still rose from parts of the little settlement. A sense of dread almost overpowered her but curiosity and the idea that she might be able to salvage things of value that she could use in her new life spurred her on. With her heart pounding in her chest and prepared to flee at any moment should danger present itself, she approached the buildings slowly and with great caution, but all was quiet. In fact, the eerie stillness was more terrifying than the darkness. She moved past the first dwelling and climbed through the window of the house that had once been her home. The roof had been completely consumed by the flames and in the pale moonlight shining down she could see a bundle lying on the floor near the fireplace. The remains of one of the rafters lay across it but when she pulled the wood away, the bundle rolled over revealing the burnt and blackened face of her grandmother. With a scream, Caitlin turned and blindly ran from the building, tripping over an obstruction that lay beside the doorway. It was another body, this time of her Father, his head twisted at an impossible angle and with a gaping wound to his throat. With no further thought of collecting items from the houses and in a state of utter confusion, Caitlin turned and ran. Ran from the terrors of the village away up the mountainside just as fast as her legs would carry her, oblivious to gasping breath or burning thighs, back to the safety of the cave. When she reached her hiding place she went straight to the furthest recess she could find, buried herself in the old plaid and burst into tears.

She lay there for the rest of that night, all the next day and the following night, neither eating nor drinking. Visions of the past day became the nightmares of her sleep; several times she awoke sweating and shaking. Her mind gave her little peace until just as dawn was breaking on the second morning she fell into a deep sleep, mostly from exhaustion but also from mental shut down as her brain could cope no more. Her sheltered upbringing in this lovely but remote place had given her little preparation for the horrors she had just encountered.

When Caitlin awoke some hours later, the terror and nightmares of the previous two days had dissipated to a point where she was now capable of some rational thought despite the sense of overwhelming emptiness. Although half child, half woman, Caitlin was a person of great courage and determination; a sense of justice had always been a large part of her character. So when she crawled to the front of the cave to the point where she could observe the glen below without being seen herself and could see for the first time the full extent of the destruction and desolation that the 'soldiers' had brought to her home and her village, she was outraged. In her emotions the terror became anger which in its turn was replaced by a great coldness.

"I don't know why they have done this to us, but I do know that it is wicked and wrong. I am the only one of my family left, so it is up to me to avenge the deaths of my grandmother, my father and my uncle and to ensure that my family regains its rightful place in this glen."

Although she didn't actually say these words, little by little over the next few weeks while the raw memories were still fresh in her mind, particularly at moments of great loneliness and homesickness for the people and places that had been taken from her, a great determination grew within her. The need for its fulfilment settled upon her in a way that would have huge influences on many of her thoughts and actions throughout the rest of her life.

CHAPTER TWO

As glens go, Glen Ceitlein is not very big. Just three miles long it runs quite steeply down into the much larger and more impressive valley that is Glen Etive, rather like the tributary of a river, which of course it originally was, but that river had been of ice during the last great ice age some ten thousand years ago. Glen Etive had become a great trade route across the Highlands of Scotland over the last two hundred years or so. The lower part of this thirty mile long valley becomes the tidal Loch Etive which allowed boats, by far the most efficient mode of transport, to bring large quantities of goods from the west coast and beyond. With no steep ascents to impede their journey but similarly, no track or road wide enough to permit the passage of carts or carriages, strings of heavily laden pack horses would convey the cargoes that had been unloaded from the vessels and up Glen Etive to a meeting point on Rannoch Moor. There they could be exchanged with goods from traders who had travelled many miles from other parts of the region. Most of these locations throughout the region have now disappeared without trace, but one; where the roads from Glen Coe and Glen Etive meet, exists to this day. The Kings House hotel still provides warmth and sustenance for the weary traveller, though it is unlikely that much trading takes place there nowadays.

Pulling herself together, Caitlin took a deep breath and began making preparations for her next move. A drink, a wash in the freezing water of the waterfall and eating the last remnants of the oat cake from the little box, she sadly reflected that there was nobody left now who would be able to replace them. She tidied her bedraggled clothes as best she could and set off down the mountain towards the big frightening world that lay before her. She had no idea what she was going to do but knew instinctively that just to survive she had to have help from other people, so she headed towards the only place she knew where she could hope to find this assistance, albeit from strangers.

Leaving Glen Ceitlein behind, she headed down into Glen Etive, to the packhorse road, which wound its way beside the river up to Rannoch Moor. In reality this little track was no more than a wide footpath, in places churned to mud by the hooves of the passing horses, Upon reaching it, Caitlin settled down on a small rock in the shelter of some bushes to await her destiny. It was raining again, that fine drenching rain that reaches every part of the body but she was oblivious to it all.

Several hours passed and Caitlin had almost given up hope of anybody coming by when she heard the faint jingling of horses' harness coming from further up the glen. Ten minutes or so later, a string of about a dozen pack horses and mules came into view, winding its way down the rocky, muddy path, each attached to the one in front by a short rein which allowed them all to be controlled by the one man who was accompanying the train. The animals were heavily laden, though not excessively so and walked at a steady pace that seemed rather slow, but if it was maintained, it would enable them to cover quite long distances in a day.

Although he wore roughly the same style of plaid as most of the men in the region, the man who was leading the first horse in the train appeared somewhat different. He was a tall man, thick set but not fat, with a mass of thick wiry black hair quite unlike the usual sandy or ginger colour that is so common among the Celtic Scots. He walked with a spring in his step and had an air of confidence about him that gave the impression that he was a man of some importance. He was, or rather his parents were Irish, who had moved from County Cork when he was a young boy to engage in the trading of horses, imported from their homeland to supply the needs of the Jacobite rebels.

Caitlin stood up and moved to stand beside the packhorse trail. She was very aware that this would probably be the only chance that she would get to receive help that day. She stood still with her head bowed and waited for the man and his animals to approach. With a high-pitched whistle which allowed even the horses at the rear of the column to hear his commands, Connor O'Driscoll brought the train to a standstill and halted beside the girl.

"And what do we have here?" Connor asked, rhetorically.

Without raising her head, Caitlin replied.

"Please sir, will you help me?"

"And what kind of trouble might you be in to need my help young lady?"

Caitlin raised her eyes to meet those of the man who stood before her.

"The soldiers came and burned our house and they killed my grandmother and my father and Uncle Iain and took everybody else away and I don't know where they are and they didn't find me, because I was up the mountain when they came." Then, after a moments pause. "And I am so hungry".

The words came tumbling out in a great rush and without any intention two large tears ran down her dirty cheeks.

This picture of a dishevelled teenage girl in tattered clothes standing beside the trail was indeed a moving sight. That she was asking for his help couldn't fail to stir his emotions and the two tears running down that beautiful young face brought a great lump to his throat. Turning away to hide his feelings and to give himself a moment to regain his composure, Connor moved beside his lead horse and without saying a word he undid the buckle that secured the flap on the saddlebag, reached in and drew out a grimy cloth bundle from which he produced some coarse barley bread and a piece of dried salt fish. Handing these to Caitlin he said.

"This is all I have to offer you young lady, but I'm happy to share it with you."

"Thank you sir," mumbled Caitlin, her mouth already full of bread.

"I'm not a Sir and never will be." The man replied with a chuckle. My name is Connor O'Driscoll but most people call me Mr Connor. And a great many other things besides I dare say though none I would like to repeat. And what is your name? And where have you come from?"

"I'm Caitlin, Caitlin Munroe." She replied. "I live in the little glen over there, but I cannot go back because the houses are burned and everyone has gone."

Mr Connor thought for a moment. He knew of several other settlements in the area that had been destroyed in a similar manner, and realised that this young girl could not survive on her own without help. He knew he couldn't leave her beside the trail, so to give himself time to try and think out the best course of action to ensure her safety, he decided that she must accompany him on his onward journey.

"Come lassie let us be on our way. We must eat as we travel, for I have to meet with the boat at the head of the loch before nightfall and if the tide is right, she will sail. Willie Mathieson will wait for no man."

Giving another whistle to his horses, this time much more low pitched, Mr Connor and the long train of horses began to move slowly forwards down the trail, the girl falling in step beside him still chewing on the last piece of fish.

For some time they travelled in silence, the man still considering his alternatives. Caitlin finished the final crumbs of food and wisely waited for him to speak first.

When finally Mr Connor broke the silence, it was in a friendly, almost fatherly tone that he spoke to Caitlin.

"It seems to me that you are definitely in need of some help young lady, but I spend most of my life on the roads and trails all over this part of Scotland. I rarely stop in a place for more than one night at a time. The market taverns where I go to get work for my horses are no place for a young girl either. So, if you are agreeable, I will take you down to the loch head and ask Willie Mathieson who is the captain of the wee vessel that brings the loads for me to take to Rannoch, to take you on the next part of your journey which will be to Oban, where I am acquainted with a person who will know what to do with you. He is the minister there, so you should be safe with him for a while."

He was completely unaware that since he had last met his clerical friend, there had been great changes to the unfortunate man's life that would make his household a totally unsuitable place for any young girl to live. However there was no doubt that when he suggested this he really did have Caitlin's best interests at heart.

"Thank you, Mr Connor."

Caitlin was still rather in awe of the stranger even though he seemed friendly enough, but her experiences over the last two days had taught her that she couldn't trust anybody and she was ready to run away at the least suspicion of aggression towards her. What she didn't know however was that this was the last thing on Mr Connor's mind for he had once had a daughter who, had she lived, would have been about the same age as Caitlin, but she had died of smallpox some years before. His wife had been a victim of the same epidemic and this tragic destruction of his family was part of the reason that he had taken to the nomadic life of the packhorse trails. Countless miles over the rough, muddy tracks of the mountains of northern Scotland and quite a few sore heads after drinking himself into a stupor in the taverns had done little to dull the pain of his loss, though time was beginning to cloud his memories. Far from being any kind of threat to her, he was sad that he could not keep her with him, but realised that it would be impossible; and it wouldn't bring his wife or daughter back.

Mr Connor asked Caitlin a few questions about her home in Glen Ceitlein and the expulsion of her family from the village, though she could tell him little more than she already had, so for the most part they walked in silence that was broken only by the jingling of the horse's harnesses and the rhythmic sound of their hooves as they squelched along the muddy trail or clattered over the rocky sections.

It took the travellers about three hours to reach the place where the land of the glen ended and salt water from the sea filled the valley even though they were some twenty miles inland. The rain had ceased and the soft autumn colours of the trees and bracken sparkled wetly in the early afternoon sunshine.

Drawn up upon a little beach and left high and dry by the falling tide, close to where the tumbling waters of the River Etive entered the tidal loch was a large boat. She could be rowed by four men and when the wind was light or in the wrong direction, the oars enabled them to continue towards their destination; but it was hard work, and wherever possible the battered lugsail was hoisted on her stumpy mast for assistance. Although not a speedy craft she was strongly built, extremely seaworthy and could withstand some of the roughest seas that would have driven many other craft scurrying for shelter. She was not a beautiful boat but had the capacity to carry an enormous quantity of cargo for her size and was ideally suited to sailing these inland lochs or the unpredictable coastal waters of the west coast of Scotland.

Another train of packhorses similar to those belonging to Mr Connor was standing on the beach alongside the boat. They were already burdened with cargo that had been transferred from the vessel to their packs for onward transportation. The loads they had brought down from the moor had been stowed aboard. At the top of the beach above the high tide mark, within a ring of smooth stones, a small fire was burning and suspended over it on a sturdy iron tripod was a large iron cooking pot. Two dogs of dubious pedigree, no doubt delighted to be onshore, were getting under the feet of the horses and of the five men working around the vessel and as a result, were getting roundly cursed in the process.

As Mr Connor, Caitlin and the horses of the pack train approached they were greeted with shouts of welcome and jokingly sarcastic comments asking where they had been and what had taken them so long. The dogs started barking, the horses hesitated then collided with one another and for a few minutes there was glorious confusion whilst the men struggled to disentangle the ropes that kept the horses tied together.

When order had finally been restored and the last remaining horses of the pack train standing beside the boat had been loaded, the boat crew, the leader of the other pack team and Mr Connor gathered round the little fire. The addition of dry gorse twigs followed by driftwood made the flames blaze up and surround the blackened pot, the contents of which were soon smelling delicious. Caitlin hung back a little, unaccustomed as she was to being in the presence of so many strangers, trying to hide some of her shyness by remaining partially concealed behind one of the pack horses but peering around its hindquarters to see what was actually going on. This was an indication of her natural curiosity that was to stand her in good stead on many occasions in the future but also to cause her a lot of trouble at other times when she should have controlled her inquisitiveness.

Mr Connor called to her and with a wave of his hand beckoned her over to the fire.

"And look what I found as I came down the glen". He said to his companions as the girl approached.

The men moved around a little and made space for Caitlin to warm herself beside the fire. She was introduced to the group and her story was told. There was sympathy and disgust at the brutality of the eviction, but not surprise, as most of them knew of recent similar happenings not too far away.

Mr Connor drew one of the boatmen aside in order to discuss Caitlin's onward journey. He was the captain of the little ship, a man by the name of Captain Willie Mathieson. Indistinguishable by his clothes as the man in charge except for the faded red stocking cap he was wearing; his bearing however left nobody in any doubt about his position of command. The other men remained close to the warmth of the fire, chatting among themselves and occasionally stirring the contents of the cooking pot. As the mariner and the horseman returned to the group, the captain was seen to tuck something into his plaid, no doubt a fee for the girl's safe onward journey.

Willie soon interrupted the conversation.

"Let us eat now for we must finish the loading and be away as soon as the tide turns."

Each man produced his own earthenware bowl and wooden spoon then helped himself to some of the steaming contents of the cooking pot. There was no spare bowl, but the men shared their meal with the girl, dipping large chunks of bread into the broth for her to eat. The stew consisted of roughly chopped turnips and potatoes, barley grain and some unidentifiable meat; most likely venison belonging to one of the hated English aristocracy, that had no doubt been killed illegally by the boat's crew on land. But Caitlin didn't know and certainly didn't care. It was food and it tasted delicious.

When all had been consumed, the bowls and the cooking pot were washed in the loch and the fire extinguished, the train of packhorses that had been beside the boat when Caitlin and Mr Connor had arrived, departed back up the track into Glen Etive. Aided by Mr Connor, Willie Mathieson and his men set to work and relieved the waiting horses of their loads and replaced their burdens with other goods as they were discharged from the boat. Most of the packs that were loaded onto the horses for the long climb up onto Rannoch Moor would have consisted of salt fish but there may well have been iron for tools and weapons from the iron smelting works at Bonawe further down the loch. Some of them could have been carrying pottery or any of the other essentials for life in the mountains that could not be produced from the thin soil or made by the local inhabitants. Occasionally there would be a small consignment of whisky from the recently opened distillery in Oban.

Before departing, Mr Connor called Caitlin over to him and laid his hand gently upon her shoulder.

"I must leave now, young lady, Willie maybe a bit dour, but he is a good man and you can trust him. You can trust Kevin Baillie in Oban too; he will be able to help you better than I."

"Thank you Mr Connor," replied Caitlin.

With final good wishes, Mr Connor and his heavily laden animals set off back up the glen along the trail by which they had come. He had a heavy heart, but was consoled by the knowledge that he was certain that he was doing the right thing for Caitlin. His encounter with this vulnerable girl had re-awoken memories of his own wife and daughter, visions that he had thought were long laid to rest within his mind. He was glad that he was alone with his horses so that there was nobody to see the hot, salty tears that flowed across his tanned cheeks to disappear into the darkness of his beard.

Caitlin watched them go and as the last horse disappeared into the trees, she felt a moment of panic that she had lost a friend even though she had only known him for a few short hours. She felt alone and frightened once again. The darkness of an unknown future filled her with dread.

CHAPTER THREE

I f Mr Connor was a man of few words, Willie Mathieson spoke even less and when he did it was mostly to bark orders to his long suffering crew. He was not an unpleasant character but failed to see the necessity to engage in conversation unless it was absolutely essential.

Pointing to a tree trunk washed up on the high tide line, probably years ago and now stripped of its bark and bleached almost white with the sun and the salt he said to the bewildered girl,

"Sit and wait."

Caitlin complied and, moving over to the indicated tree, sat down on a convenient branch and watched until the four men had stowed all the remaining cargo that had been lying on the shore aboard the little vessel and covered it with an old sail for protection. The pack train could have brought almost anything down to the little boat, bales of cloth from the jute and linen mills of Dundee, powder and musket balls, books, leather or any of the other things that had to be brought from far away. In actual fact, all of Mr Connor's animals had been carrying grain. The west coast of Scotland is not particularly suited to cereal production, so the sacks of barley would be made into bannocks, the flat unleavened bread that, other than porridge, which could be produced from locally grown oats, was the staple diet of the people of the glens.

With the rising tide now lapping round the bow, the boat was almost afloat when Willie came over to Caitlin where she was sitting on the tree and without a word, scooped her up in his arms, waded out alongside the boat and dumped her unceremoniously over the side onto the little deck beside the mast. Willie Mathieson moved to the bow and with a final push the boat floated. As soon as she did so, he scrambled aboard and using their oars as poles, the crew pushed their little ship away from the land into deeper water.

Once clear of the shore, they turned her bow until it was pointing seawards and with all of the men except Willie hauling on the halyard, they hoisted the tan coloured mainsail to take advantage of the steady breeze that had sprung up and was blowing down the loch.

With the crew occupied in getting the boat under way, they took little notice of Caitlin so she moved up into the bows where she would not get under anybody's feet. Tucked away in a little cubbyhole beside the bowsprit she found an old and rather smelly tarpaulin sheet. Partly to keep out of the way and partly to keep warm she crawled under its shelter. With her back against the stout, old wooden planking, she laid back, her head cradled on the crook of her elbow and listened to the swish of the water being thrust aside by the little ships passage. One of the dogs that had been creating havoc on the beach came to investigate what was under the tarpaulin and, satisfied that she was friendly, crawled in beside her. Taking comfort from the reassuring sounds of the men's voices coming from the stern of the boat and from the warm furry creature curled up beside her, Caitlin felt that she was safe at least for the time being and with this security and a full stomach, she promptly fell asleep. But despite being exhausted, her mind would not rest and her sleep was disturbed by meaningless dreams, dreams that were full of incoherent images of the distressing things that she had witnessed in the last few days; disjointed visions of men running, people screaming and of her own breath coming in great gasps as she climbed desperately away from something or someone she did not know.

Sometime later, though how long she had no idea, she was woken by the unfamiliar sensations of the boat pitching and rolling about in the rough seas. Never having travelled beyond the head of the loch before, she had no concept of waves in the open sea. Fear gripped her once more as she poked her head out from under the canvas to find that it was pitch dark, the night sky covered in a million twinkling stars. That was all she saw because almost as soon as she had looked upwards her face was immediately showered with splashes of cold salt spray. She did not want to get soaked again but, as she was about to crawl back under the tarpaulin she looked up and was comforted by the calm and reassuring silhouette of Willie Mathieson as he stood at the tiller, dark and solid against the paler water of the little boat's wake. Retreating under the cover again, she wiped the salty water from her face with the corner of her plaid, and crawled back into the warmth of where she had been before; she lay there trembling for a while until sleep overcame her once again.

When next she woke, the uneasy motion of the boat she had felt the previous night had gone and almost before she could move, the tarpaulin was pulled back to reveal Willie Mathieson's bewhiskered but not unkindly face looking down at her.

"Come," he said.

Caitlin scrambled to her feet. She rubbed her eyes to try to chase away the last remnants of sleep and looked around her. Dawn had broken and the little vessel was now moored alongside a crude stone jetty that curved halfway across the mouth of a deep bay, its protection effectively forming a large harbour sheltered from the seaward side. Gently sloping hills covered in trees formed one side of the bay, offering shelter from the land. A large burn or small river ran into the sea, babbling across the stones of the beach rather than making its own channel. Perhaps a dozen low-built stone cottages with thatched roofs lined the shore of the inlet. They were not more than a few yards from the high-tide line with only a broad pathway to separate the dwellings from the sand itself. In front of them a number of small boats were drawn up on the beach; most were upturned, the black tarred bottoms of their hulls resembling a row of beached whales. On the other side of the harbour, just below the rocky bluff that formed the opposite arm of protection for this haven, was a large slightly sinister-looking building, two storeys high with a great slate roof and a tall brick chimney. This, Caitlin was told later, was the whisky distillery that had been built some eight years before and its presence in the settlement was already changing what had once been a small fishing village into a prosperous port. And so it is to this day.

On the shore, close to where the jetty left the beach and entered the sea, stood a huge stack of several hundred dirty wicker baskets filled with charcoal, prepared by the depredation of thousands of ancient trees cut from the surrounding Caledonian forest, destined for the furnaces of the ironworks at Bonawe. These baskets were awaiting shipment in boats similar to the one which had brought Caitlin to this little town of Oban. Before many more years had passed, this charcoal production would have destroyed almost all of the great, natural Caledonian forest and although imported coal would replace the charcoal as a source of heat for a while, the iron smelting industry would also decline and disappear altogether within the next few decades.

Set back a little from the shoreline of the bay, on a small rise in the land just to one side of the burn, there was a tiny church. Only slightly bigger than the cottages, it could be distinguished from the dwelling houses by the little tower above the roof at one end, in which had been placed a small exposed bell. The white painted walls caused it to stand out against the green hillsides behind, and as soon as it had been built some thirty years before it had become an excellent landmark for the fishing boats coming in from the sea. A robust, square, stone house, not much smaller than the church had been erected next door. Built of smooth-cut square stone blocks, two stories high and roofed in grey slates rather than the traditional turf or heather thatch of the other cottages, its dour and slightly foreboding aspect made it stand out from all the fishermens' cottages This was the residence of the minister. The strict and uncompromising teachings of the Calvinistic Church of Scotland allowed little room for any architectural adornment in any buildings, least of all in the accommodation for the servants of the church itself; the minister and his family.

It was raining again with a cold, damp wind blowing in from the sea as Caitlin Munroe and Willie Mathieson walked down the jetty to the shore and along the muddy, unpaved road towards the cottages. Although the soles of her feet were very tough, she was unused to walking on stony roads, as there had been none at all in the glen, only flat rock, mud and vegetation, so she tried to pick her way around the roughest places, but at the same time keep up with the big man. It was obviously no use trying to talk to or ask questions of Willie Mathieson who seemed intent on relieving himself of his charge as soon as possible. He walked at such a pace that Caitlin had to trot after him whenever they came to a smoother part of the path. Keeping his head bent low and his face turned away from the rain Willie Mathieson paid no heed to the girl behind, presumably, simply expecting her to follow him. Not a soul was stirring outside any of the fishermen's cottages at this early hour, though a thin plume of smoke was starting to appear from the chimneys of several as the peat fires within were stirred back into life at the beginning of the day. They hurried past all the cottages and continued on as the road turned away from the beach and up the gentle rise until they reached the house beside the little white church.

Pointing to the dry-stone wall that surrounded the meagre front garden, Willie Mathieson ordered Caitlin to 'sit', whilst he walked to the front door and, raising the horseshoe-shaped doorknocker, rapped sharply several times. There was no reply until, after the fourth assault upon the door, it was opened a tiny crack, just wide enough for half a face to become visible. Following some discussion with the unseen person inside, the door opened fully, the visitor was admitted and closed again behind him. Although the girl was warm after her vigorous walk, and her plaid was designed to shield her from most weathers, the cold and the wetness had slowly begun to seep through her clothing. She sat on the cold stone of the wall for what seemed to be an eternity but was probably no more than ten minutes and, knowing full well that her destiny was being decided for her inside the house, her terror began to return, until, just as she was about to run away again, away from her fear of the unknown, the door re-opened and Willie Mathieson stood in the opening, beckoning her forward into the house. The front door slammed shut behind her and she stood on the door mat, a very bedraggled sight with water streaming down her face and shivering with cold. A man and a woman stood next to Willie Mathieson facing her and before she could absorb any of the detail of the room within, Willie Mathieson spoke.

"This is the Reverend Baillie and Mrs Baillie. They will be looking after you now."

Without another word, without even a glance at the girl, Willie Mathieson walked straight past her, strode from the house and out of her life forever. In a strange sort of way, Willie Mathieson had a profound impact on Caitlin, although he had made only a fleeting appearance in her life, she often remembered his weather beaten face and his taciturn nature, linked with his ability to command others almost without speaking. This was probably her first experience of men doing another's bidding from respect rather than fear or parental obedience.

CHAPTER FOUR

The couple before whom Caitlin stood could not have been more different from each other. The minister, Kevin Baillie was a short, stout man with a pleasant face that was almost entirely hidden by a huge ginger beard. The buttons of his waistcoat were under considerable strain from within and the woolly slippers on his feet just did not seem to fit with the rest of his clothing, which was clean, dark and sombre. Although he was at least twice the weight of his wife, it was obvious who the dominant one of the couple was.

In complete contrast to her husband, Enid Baillie was a tall, skinny woman with dark hair that was turning to grey, wound into a tight knot at the back of her head. Her plain, floor length dress was unadorned except for a starched white collar fastened firmly round her neck. Her face was long with her nose and chin sharp and pointed. Her eyelids always seemed half closed as though she was scrutinising every move and she only ever opened them fully when she was angry. Caitlin would soon learn to dread those dark eyes that always seemed so full of malevolence.

After a moment or two, having looked the shivering girl up and down, the woman sniffed.

"Well, I suppose we had better do something with you if we've got to have you here. Come."

Totally ignoring her husband and without giving him a chance to speak, Mrs Baillie turned on her heel and swept out of the room with just the faintest jerk of her head to indicate to Caitlin that she was to follow. The doorway led into a drab looking room at the back of the house that served as a scullery. The older woman poured some cold water from a wooden bucket into a large pottery sink, handed her a bar of grey, gritty soap and a small piece of coarse cloth to use as a towel. She told Caitlin to strip and wash herself all over, while she went to find her something dry to wear.

Caitlin did as she was told, even though the water was freezing and the soap so hard it was almost impossible to create any sort of lather. When Mrs Baillie returned, she immediately thrust some clothing at the girl, saying in a cold, harsh tone.

"Cover yourself with this girl. Don't ever let me see you unclothed again. Now give me those old rags and when you have dressed, you may come to the kitchen where I will show you what you have to do."

The dress that Caitlin had been given was an old cast-off from Mrs Baillie's limited wardrobe. Of charcoal grey, worn thin to the point of being threadbare it fitted Caitlin's more youthful but fuller figure, but only just. And it was terribly scratchy. Designed to be worn with an undergarment, which had not been provided, its coarse fibres chafed her young skin dreadfully, making her long for the soft wool of her plaid and shawl. After a few days of discomfort, she asked for her old clothes back but her request was flatly refused and her mistress told her that they were so disgusting that she had thrown them away, though Caitlin found them some weeks later, discarded in an old basket in the shed behind the house.

When Caitlin entered the kitchen, Mrs Baillie was standing in front of the open fire stirring something in a large pot that was suspended on a chain hanging down from the chimney. She didn't hear the girl arrive, so Caitlin had a moment to look around her.

The stone walls had been whitewashed and the rough stone floor was clean; there were some plain wooden cupboards against the walls and a table with a white scrubbed pine top in the centre of the room. The only available light came from a small window set high up in the wall; so high that nothing could be seen but sky. The stark appearance and the inability to see anything out of the window made the room feel like a prison cell. A cold chill of foreboding descended upon the girl; how little did she know that her worst and deepest fears were soon to be realised. That dismal room with its unfriendly high window was to assume great prominence in the dark dreams and nightmares that would fill her disturbed and fitful sleep in the months to come.

When the minister's wife turned from the fire and saw Caitlin standing there, she gave a small gasp of surprise but instantly regained her composure and glared angrily at the newcomer.

"Don't ever creep up on me again girl." she shouted. "Or I will throw you out of this house instantly. No matter what Mr Connor might say."

What Mr Connor had done to create such influence on the household, Caitlin never discovered, but whatever it was, for Enid Baillie to dare to include it in a threat like that, it was undoubtedly meant to strike terror into the girl.

"Seeing as we are obliged to have you here, you might as well be useful, so listen carefully and do as you are told or I will make your life such a misery that you will wish you never saw the sight of Oban!"

"First of all, you will address me as Ma'am or Mrs Baillie at all times."

Mrs Baillie then told Caitlin in a very condescending way what tasks she was expected to perform throughout the day and what she could and couldn't do whilst she was in the house. Caitlin just stood with her head down, her mind in a complete turmoil. Most of what the other woman said to her just didn't make any sense. The little house in the glen had been so simple; just one room with a fire in the middle and a small area beside it curtained off for sleeping. The cattle were kept in one end of the building, partitioned off from the family but sharing the same doorway. Even though it was the end of the eighteenth century, life in these remote places in Scotland was quite primitive and probably hadn't changed a great deal for several hundred years. Though the people that lived there were fairly happy, it was a far cry from the puritanical, almost antiseptic orderliness of the house of a Church of Scotland minister. Caitlin wanted to ask so many questions but was afraid that whatever she asked would just bring her more trouble and scolding. So she said nothing.

A bowl of thin, grey, watery porridge was thrust into her hands with the order to hurry up and eat it because she was needed to fetch some water from the burn. Nobody told her where the best place was to access the water, so as she stooped to fill her wooden bucket from the burn, the front of her dress dipped into the swirling water and the force of the current nearly dragged her off her feet. The heavy wooden bucket, rapidly filling with the rushing water was torn from her frozen fingers. Only the opportune presence of a low-growing rowan tree sprouting bravely from the rocky bank meant that she was able to maintain her balance. She just succeeded in grasping one of the slender branches which prevented her from being swept away in the fast-moving current. Fortunately the bucket did not travel downstream very far before becoming wedged on the rocks at the top of the beach and Caitlin was able to recover it, thankfully undamaged though it did make her take longer than her Mistress had been expecting. Upon her return to the house, her dress soaked, she was subjected to the most dreadful harangue from Mrs Baillie who informed her, at the top of her voice that she was a useless idiot and that the sooner she left the house the better it would be for all concerned.

This was the beginning of the most awful time of Caitlin's life. Whatever she did and no matter how hard she tried to please her benefactor, she would always be in the wrong and was informed of such in no uncertain terms. Many times she had her knuckles rapped for not using her knife and fork properly, at others she went to bed hungry for doing or not doing something of which she had no knowledge. Her bed was only a pile of discarded clothes and curtains on the hard wooden floor, up in the cold of the attic just under the leaky slate roof. Her existence was little better than slavery; no mention was ever made of any sort of payment, and if Enid Baillie thought there was any chance that the poor girl's tasks would be completed sooner than anticipated, giving her some free time, she simply imposed some extra work or criticised what she was already doing and forced her to do the work all over again.

But she had no choice; she had nowhere to run away to, and had no idea how to find something better. She learned fast and she learned the hard way. Little did she know that this period of hardship and suffering was giving her a toughness and resilience that would stand her in good stead in times to come.

Not only were the usual household chores, of cleaning, washing, tending the fires and preparing food, though not actually the cooking, demanded of her, but also any other menial task that her mistress could find for her to do. Looking back on this time many years later, Caitlin realised that these extra impositions were just another way that the vindictive Minister's wife found to exert her sadistic power over the girl as often as she possibly could. As is the way of most bullies Enid Bailie probably took great pleasure in being able to command and punish someone weaker and less able than herself.

Perhaps the hardest task that she was made to do was to fetch the peats for the fire. These had been dug from the boggy ground of the high moors then stacked to dry. They had to be carried on her

31

back to the house in a wicker basket with leather carrying straps that cut cruelly into her young shoulders. This was an arduous journey of more than two miles on rough, often steep, stony tracks and she had to make this trip several times a week, regardless of the weather. In the short, cold days of autumn, she would often not get back to the house with her heavy load until well after darkness had fallen. This labour did however have the compensation of allowing her a brief period out of earshot of her benefactress's vicious tongue and biting sarcasm.

By the time she had finished all the work that had been allotted to her, Caitlin was much too exhausted to explore the little town, not that she would have dared to for she had been strictly forbidden to leave the immediate vicinity of the house, garden or church, except for her trips to the peat diggings and even then she was told never to speak to anyone she might meet.

Caitlin did not complain, although many were the nights when she cried herself to sleep, she realised only too well that any form of rebellion or protest would only make things worse, and anyway, she had been brought up in an environment where you just did not question the orders of adults, particularly your parents. Unfortunately, the absence of objection only seemed to inspire Enid Baillie to impose even more labour on the already overworked girl; indeed, only a week or so after Caitlin's arrival she was given the additional labour of scrubbing the hard, cold stone floor of the little church next door. This was an unforgiving task because the pathways around the outside of the church were unpaved and any visitor to the building always left a trail of muddy footprints across the floor.

There was however an incident that occurred in the church whilst she was engaged in this thankless task that would have a considerable effect on Caitlin's future, though of course she did not know it at the time.

One evening, just as it was beginning to get dark Caitlin was wiping away the last of the dirty water from the floor in the furthest, darkest corner of the church, conveniently, as it happened, as far away from the entrance as she could be when she heard the creak of the door opening and footsteps quickly cross her newly-cleaned floor. Rather than make her presence known and suspecting that it was her mistress coming to harangue her again, the girl, who was already on her hands and knees, kept low and just peeped around the base of a pillar to see who it was. Sure enough, it was Mrs Baillie who had entered the building but rather than approach the altar as she would usually have done, instead, she walked straight across to the pulpit, which was little more than a built-in lectern. Completely unaware that she was being observed, the minister's wife knelt on the floor, pulled away the wooden board at the base of the small step and having reached into the pocket of her apron, thrust something into the cavity below the step before pushing the board back into its original position. Swiftly, the woman rose and, brushing any tell-tale marks from the front of her dress, turned and left the church without a backward glance.

Although she was bursting with curiosity, Caitlin did not immediately rush and see what had been hidden underneath the pulpit but completed drying the floor as if nothing had happened. Having listened carefully for a minute to make sure that her persecutor had not returned, she rose to her feet and hurried across the church to where she had seen the other woman conceal whatever it was. She had some difficulty working out how to release the board that covered the hiding place but eventually she was successful and, putting her hand into the cavity she withdrew a small, cloth, drawstring bag. She didn't even have to open it to know what was inside; the contents were quite heavy and chinked in the way only coins can.

Now she knew that it was money that had been concealed, Caitlin did not bother to open the bag or try to count the money, the different coins meant nothing to her anyway, but hurriedly thrust the bag back where she had found it, replaced the wooden board and, picking up her water bowl, floor cloth and scrubbing brush, hurried unseen, out of the church and back to the house where she busied herself with some of the other tasks she had to complete before nightfall. It wasn't until she met Mrs Baillie coming into the kitchen from the parlour at the same time as she was entering with a basket of peats from the stack outside and when her mistress never even bothered to speak to her, she felt confident that the other woman had no idea that she had been observed during her clandestine visit to the church.

Kevin Baillie's character was largely in accordance with his appearance. He was a genial man who tried to make Caitlin's life, as far as it was possible, at least tolerable, taking into account the attitude and actions of the woman his wife had become. He had been a happy-go-lucky child who was always to be seen running round the poorer streets of Dundee, where he was born. He was fearless, with absolutely no sense of danger, but when he was only eight years old, a dare with one of his pals had gone seriously wrong. Whilst trying to jump from one cartload of jute bales to another as they passed each other on the way from the docks to the processing mills he had slipped and fallen under the huge, iron-shod wheels of a horse drawn cart. The severe injuries to both feet caused him a great deal of pain throughout his life and prevented him from wearing ordinary shoes. This accident, for which he only had himself to blame and the fact that he could only walk short distances had completely changed the direction his life had taken.

With disabilities such as his, in normal circumstances, life would have been a rapid descent into poverty that would, almost certainly, have resulted in a short miserable existence of dependence on alcohol and begging on the streets dressed in rags. He was saved from this degradation and misery by the kindly intervention of the minister of the local church who recognised in the lad, a clever brain in an injured body, that needed assistance. The clergyman had taken the crippled lad under his own roof, fed him, clothed him and given him sufficient education to make him realise that there was a future for someone with injuries such as his.

Kevin had rewarded the foresight and perception of this charitable gentleman with a diligence and a gratitude which drove him to complete a successful education. The hard work and dedication finally led to his ordination and his acceptance of the ministry of The Presbyterian church in Oban. This boyhood accident was the reason why he had been wearing incongruous woolly slippers when Caitlin had first been introduced to him. His incapacity also meant that he was unable to travel round his parish as much as he would have liked, so he too had to endure considerable periods of verbal abuse from his wife.

For reasons he did not fully understand or Enid had chosen not to divulge, Kevin and his wife had been unable to have any children of their own, a great sadness to the minister, and probably to his wife also, (though she would never admit it). Perhaps in Caitlin he saw a daughter he would have wished for, so he did his best to make her burden as light as possible, a friendly smile, a fatherly pat on the shoulder when he knew his wife was elsewhere. But he was no match for his wife. Bible stories or even just ordinary day-to-day conversation were not permitted to get in the way of the drudgery that was Caitlin's lot from dawn to dusk. How she wished for her old life back in the glen where, once the daily chores had been accomplished she was free to go wherever she wished and to play with the other children from the neighbouring cottages; or when it was dark, she could sit beside the glowing peat fire and listen to the tales that her father would tell. But it could not be. It was gone forever.

CHAPTER FIVE

About a month after she had arrived at the minister's house Mrs Baillie summoned Caitlin into the little parlour, a room that she was not normally permitted to enter, except to clean the floor or to empty the cold ashes from the fireplace early in the morning. The Minister, looking most uncomfortable and uneasy, and his wife were standing in front of the fire, with the woman looking more displeased than usual. In the most hostile tone imaginable, Mrs Baillie said.

"After you came to us, it seemed that the best way to deal with the unfortunate situation of your arrival was to despatch you to the poorhouse in Glasgow as soon as possible. Consequently, my husband wrote to the superintendent there requesting your immediate admittance. However, it seems that there are a huge number of other orphans in need of his charity; no doubt as a consequence of the wicked, illegal and immoral activity of the English. Thus the superintendent was unable to agree to our request."

Enid Baillie paused to allow the full drama and dreadfulness of the moment to sink deep into the poor girl's heart then continued.

"So it seems that we will have to suffer your presence here for the foreseeable future, however unpleasant that will be for both the Reverend and myself. It is the mysterious Will of the Lord that those who seek to serve Him should be made to suffer for their goodwill to all men. It would seem that our dedication to the Lord means that we must even provide for the children of those who are so feckless that they cannot, or will not, provide for their own children but prefer to continue on their Godless path of filth and fornication towards their own eternal damnation. We do not want you here. You are a scourge upon our God-fearing household. You will remain here, but only until we can find an alternative place for you to live. Now go and return to your tasks."

Although Caitlin heard these words, she had no idea what they meant. She had no concept of the meaning of the words "filth and fornication". To her, life was just that, life; she had lived from day to day without any appreciation that people could live in ways totally different to hers, she did not know what decadence or depravity meant. Her parents were certainly not guilty of the accusations that were laid against them; rather, they too had been brought up in a simple, remote region that was quietly Protestant in a God-fearing way and would never have contemplated either filth or fornication to enter their minds. Caitlin herself was completely and utterly innocent and ignorant of all ways of life other than her own. It was because of this secluded and isolated upbringing that she was being very rapidly educated in the ways of the outside world in the most painful, miserable way imaginable.

Following the announcement of Caitlin's apparent permanence of residence, Enid Baillie's attitude towards the girl became more unpleasant than ever before. She no longer treated her as some sort of servant, rather as a slave who was there to be abused and tongue-lashed at every available opportunity. If anything went astray or got broken, it would always be Caitlin's fault and there were times when verbal abuse did not seem to be sufficient and physical violence towards her became frequent. She would often be struck with the first thing that came to hand for no apparent reason or given a vicious flick with a towel across the back of the legs which often left the girl with welts and bruises. It seemed to the girl that her mistress only sent her out to fetch water from the burn or to collect peat from the diggings when it was pouring with rain; which, being western Scotland it often was! Enid Baillie was a cruel, bitter, sadistic woman who for no particular reason treated Caitlin in the most vicious ways possible.

Caitlin knew full well that she had to escape this intolerable situation as soon as possible but had no idea how she was going to achieve this. She had very little knowledge of the outside world, so she had no real means of making any sort of decision, let alone the right one.

However, providence seemed to take a hand in the wretched girl's future because some two weeks after her summons to the parlour, after a wild and stormy night, a much larger ship than would normally be seen in Oban limped into the bay, having sustained considerable damage as a result of the gale. A number of the sails had been ripped to pieces by the storm and what was left of them hung in tatters from her yards. Ropes and rigging were in a terrible tangle, several parts of the ship's rail had been washed away and the cargo had shifted, causing the vessel to list dangerously to one side. Her arrival had caused something of a sensation in the town. It was not often that the rhythms of life were affected so dramatically; usually the only craft seen were the local fishing boats, the little cargo vessels such as the one that had brought Caitlin from Glen Etive or the occasional coastal trader.

Once the gale that had caused the damage to the ship had subsided, the crew attached one end of a long rope from the vessel's bow to the end of the jetty and by using the capstan they were able to haul her up alongside the quay in readiness for repairs to begin.

Despite the bedraggled appearance of the *Maid of Eriskay*, the hull of the vessel was intact and still watertight. Her cargo of oyster shells was destined for the pottery industry of the industrial midlands of

England, where their incorporation into the glazes helped in creating the lustrous, pearlescent effect so popular at the time. Despite shifting to one side of the ship, causing her to list alarmingly the oyster shells had sustained no damage. There was little need for external assistance; all that was required was a safe haven and calm waters where the damage could be repaired before the ship continued on her way. Once the weary crew had rested, they set to, trimmed and levelled the cargo to bring the ship back onto an even keel, sorted and re-secured the rigging, repaired what sails were salvageable and replaced the others that had been destroyed completely. Finally they stretched ropes across the gaps left by the damage to the rails to ensure the safety of the crew until permanent replacements could be fitted when the ship arrived in Liverpool; her original destination.

The ship could be seen from the minister's house and when Mr Baillie just happened to mention that he had heard that the necessary repairs had been completed and the ship would sail the following morning, Caitlin decided that she must get on board somehow. Whether or not the Pastor's information was intended as a suggestion that could help her to escape from his wife's intolerable attentions Caitlin would never know, but she always liked to think that this was actually the case.

That night Caitlin lay down on her crude bed in the attic and despite being very tired after a long day's work she was far too excited, and terrified to even contemplate sleep but lay awake until all was still in the house and the last light had been extinguished. Mr Baillie's snores could be heard from the bedroom below as she crept downstairs and away from that horrid place. She paused only to change back into her old plaid and shawl, which she had secreted in the wood pile some time before. She slipped into the kitchen and gathered some leftover food from the larder and fastened it into a towel tied together by the corners to form a bag and left the house. Caitlin hurried across to the church where she managed, despite the darkness to locate the secret hiding place under the pulpit. Sliding the panel to one side, she reached in and withdrew the bag containing the coins that she had seen Mrs Baillie hide two weeks before. Caitlin never knew why her persecutor was hiding money, but when she thought about it years later, she suspected it may well have had something to do with her being able to exert some form of control over her husband. Tucking the little bag into her plaid, Caitlin slipped from the church and headed for the seashore.

Knowing that if she was caught, she would be subjected to some terrible punishment and with her heart pounding, the girl moved as silently as she could. Her bare feet were impervious to any discomfort caused by the rough boulders; she picked her way carefully along the beach until she reached the jetty alongside which the ship was moored. Expecting that at any moment dogs would bark and reveal her presence or she would be seen by a night watchman she moved as quietly as possible along the jetty, in almost pitch darkness. But all was still. A single dim light shone from the little cabin at the stern of the ship, so Caitlin scrambled over the rail as close to the bow as she could to prevent being spotted as a silhouette. Once on board, she moved away, as far as she could, from the lantern and feeling around in the inky blackness she searched for some kind of hiding place. Under a small canopy up in the bows she found a narrow space beside a deck beam that was just wide enough for her to crawl into and hopefully not be seen. Making sure that all parts of her plaid and shawl were tucked under her body so as not to betray her presence, Caitlin settled down and waited for the ship to sail and to take her away from the hellish life she had been leading. There was nothing else she could do.

It was some time during the following morning that she was discovered. The ship had put to sea several hours previously and was now sailing south between the smaller islands of the Inner Hebrides with a steady wind on her beam.

The weather was fine and the warm sunshine had brought two children up on deck to play hide and seek. The little boy of about six years old had chosen the space where Caitlin was concealed as his hiding place.

As the boy, Malcolm, slid into the confined space, he was confronted with Caitlin's pale face and wide eyes staring at him out of the gloom. With a high-pitched squeak, he shot backwards out onto the deck, almost colliding with his elder sister who had come seeking him. Grabbing the girl, Angelina, by the arm, he said breathlessly.

"There's someone in there." Pointing to the gap under the beam.

"Rubbish" replied his sister and getting down on her knees she peered into the dark recess. On seeing the same ghostly apparition, she repeated her brother's retreat at even greater speed.

"We must tell mother". Said Angelina.

Holding each other's hand more for mutual reassurance than for protection, they ran along the deck to tell their mother who was sitting in the cabin at the stern of the ship, writing a letter to her husband.

As was consistent with her nature, when Mary Blake managed to understand what her excited but apprehensive children were trying to tell her, rather than going straight to the captain, decided to investigate the situation herself. Heaving her not inconsiderable bulk out onto the deck, unbalanced by the rolling motion of the ship she moved slightly unsteadily forward until she came to the canopy in the bows.

"Now where did you see this face?" She asked her children.

Malcolm pointed to the gap under the deck beam then quickly retreated to hide behind his mother's skirts. Squeezing under the canopy, close to where Caitlin was hiding but due to her size not close enough to see whatever or whoever it was that her children had seen, Mary called out to the person in the darkness in a clear but kindly voice.

"Come out and reveal yourself. I shall do you no harm."

Frightened almost out of her wits at the prospect of what might happen next, but not really having any option, Caitlin scrambled out from her hiding place under the forecastle and came face to face with the most extraordinary woman she had ever seen. With a mass of bright red hair, several chins and the most enormous bosom, Mary was, to say the least, an imposing sight, beloved by children though nervously respected by authority; but what was most noticeable of all was the smile that never left her face and the most piercing bright blue eyes that always seemed to twinkle. Not knowing whether to hide again or to run, though on board ship, there was really nowhere to run, Caitlin just stood and stared, her mouth wide open. Mary chuckled.

"There is no need to be afraid of me my dear. I shan't hurt you. Are you hungry?"

Caitlin nodded, too amazed to speak and from somewhere deep in the folds of her clothing the ever- practical Mary produced a speckled red-green shiny apple and handed it to the girl.

"There you are, my dear. Food and drink in one."

It wasn't until she bit into the delicious fruit that Caitlin realised just how hungry she was. The food she had brought from Mrs Baillie's kitchen had been forgotten in the fear and excitement of her escape.

The apple was almost half-gone before Mary spoke again. The pause was partly to allow the stowaway to eat, but also to give the older woman time to observe the girl and to assess the situation. She had a good idea that the young girl before her, dressed in little better than rags and looking very scared, must have come from one of the dispossessed families that were scattered throughout the area as a result of what was to become known in later years as "the Highland Clearances". This bland-sounding phrase gives little clue as to the most dreadful hardship, poverty and starvation that occurred during these turbulent years and the destruction of a complete culture that ultimately caused the dispersal of many thousands of dispossessed people to all corners of the globe.

Mary's voice was soft and reassuring and yet full of confidence.

"Don't worry, my dear. You are safe with me. Now, would you like to tell me who you are and how you came to be hiding here? I will listen carefully to what you tell me and then we can decide what is the best thing to do."

Although she had met some kindly people in the weeks since she left the glen, Mr Connor and Kevin Baillie in particular, this was the first time since her life and family had been destroyed that Caitlin believed truly that this woman was someone she could trust implicitly. So suddenly, impulsively, the child in her re-emerged and she flung her arms around Mary, or rather, as far round as they would reach and burst into tears.

Mary did not hurry the girl; she just held her close and waited for the sobbing to subside. Though she didn't realise it at that time, this was the first physical contact the girl had had with another human being for several months. The children had crawled in behind their mother and were peeping round her skirts curious to see this tearful newcomer. Gently, very gently, Mary coaxed the entire story from the girl, waiting patiently whenever the memories became too painful and the tears flowed again. As she learned more and more of the details of Caitlin's recent life, her own mind was whirring, trying to work out some sort of solution to the girl's problems and how she could help her whilst being mindful of her own situation and that of the two children snuggling against her.

The best way to describe Mary Blake was to say she was 'a character'. She was a native of Fort William, a town situated at the head of Loch Linnie some forty miles north of Oban. Longer and larger than Loch Etive, Loch Linnie did not have the barrier of the Falls of Lora, a narrow gorge at the entrance with rapid, dangerous currents and whirlpools that hampered the navigation of Loch Etive. Much larger vessels could come and go at will, if the wind and tide permitted and its sheltered waters had allowed a considerable fishery to spring up with, in particular, an abundance of shellfish, especially, scallops. If kept cool and wet, these much coveted shellfish could be transported alive so it was possible for them to be distributed widely across most parts of Scotland as well as providing considerable income for the fishermen of Fort William. They were also an excellent source of food for the local population.

Mary's family had been fishermen for generations and from the time her father was permanently crippled when he was accidentally trapped between two boats when she was just fifteen years old and as an only child, Mary had no option but to take over his little fishing boat in order to provide for herself and her parents. It was almost unheard of for a female to go to sea in the fishing boats and many considered it unlucky. Women were restricted to the menial work on the shore, gutting fish, mending nets and providing home comforts for their menfolk. Mary just laughed at all this prejudice and worked extremely hard, soon becoming proficient at most of the skills she needed to take her father's place. Before long she was achieving catches almost as large as the men working on the other boats. Strapping lass that she was, she was almost as strong as many of her male counterparts and with her outgoing personality and constant good humour she soon became popular with the fishing community, gaining the respect of all the other fishermen and the townsfolk of Fort William. Mary was well known throughout the locality for her "larger than life" personality.

All this changed however when she met, and after an exciting courtship, married a sergeant in the British army who was stationed at the garrison in Fort William.

It had been considered necessary by the British government in London to establish a military presence on the west coast of

Scotland to dissuade the population from rebelling against the English. The unseemly connivance of the English parliament to the illegal and brutal 'clearances' being, no doubt, the major reason that there had been several bloody uprisings over the past fifty years. This unrest had caused considerable inconvenience to the rich and influential landlords and had necessitated considerable military resources and manpower being brought to the Highlands to bring the clans under control. The deterrent seemed to have worked because there had been very little rioting in the area for quite some time and when Sergeant Henry Blake was posted to Fort William there was very little active soldiering to do.

As an enthusiastic and diligent soldier, Sergeant Blake saw to it that his men did not become lethargic and dissolute despite the lack of excitement, and although he was continually exercising his men, it was not by harshness that he gained their respect, rather by example and fairness.

When Henry Blake heard of the phenomenon of an enormous fisherman, or rather fisherwoman with long, ginger hair, he decided to see for himself. He had been an oyster fisherman working on the fishing smacks that sailed from Whitstable in Kent for some years himself, before joining the army and well understood the rigours and hard work involved in the shellfish industry. When they actually met and he spoke with her one bright December morning down by the shores of Loch Linnie, he was totally unprepared for the reality that was Mary. The report of her size had been exaggerated somewhat, though not by much and he had been expecting the mass of red hair. What he had not anticipated however was the courtesy and femininity that shone through the external trappings of the harsh realities of the shellfish trade and no rough and well-worn fisherman's smock could hope to hide her voluptuous figure.

From the first moment he was captivated by those twinkling blue eyes. For her part, Mary found in Henry a man with a fine sense of humour and most importantly, a strong sense of duty whom she could respect and trust. Theirs was a whirlwind courtship, regulated by the tides rather than by the day and the night, and before very long they had become inseparable and began to think of a permanent future together. In the event, the wedding had to be brought forward by some months due to the unexpected but not unwelcome discovery that Mary was already expecting their first child, Angelina.

Henry Blake's leadership qualities and popularity with his men did not go unnoticed by his superiors at a time in the British army when promotion could take many years, or even decades. By the time their second child Malcolm was five years old, Henry had been promoted to lieutenant. Six months later, much to the couples sorrow, he was dispatched to Canada to command a force of Marines who were assisting the navy in their efforts to ensure the safe passage of British merchant ships entering and leaving the St. Lawrence River free from the unwelcome attentions of the French Fleet. The strategy must have been effective, as there had been very little French activity for many months and because the situation seemed fairly stable, after about a year of separation, Lieutenant Blake had sent for his wife and children to join him in St John's in Newfoundland where he was based.

As a consequence, Mary and her family were now in the process of sailing down the west coast of Scotland to Liverpool on the *Maid of Eriskay* to join a much larger vessel that would take them on the transatlantic part of their journey, or rather they were when they had encountered the severe south-westerly gale which had obliged the ship to seek a safe haven for necessary repair. Oban was the nearest "port in a storm".

CHAPTER SIX

Once Caitlin's story had been told up to the present, Mary thought in silence for a few minutes. Her children beside her had fallen asleep in the warm sunshine, snuggled in her voluminous skirts, tired from their play and the excitement of Caitlin's discovery. Finally she spoke; summing up the situation.

"Well, one thing is certain my dear. You can't go back to the glen where you came from for there is nothing and nobody left there for you to go back to. Neither can you return to Oban because your treatment by that wicked woman was little more than slavery, and you took the money. I don't consider that it was stealing, rather as wages for two months hard labour. She will be certain that you took the money but if she were to make a to-do, she would have to explain away why she had the coins there in the first place. Now, I think that you had better show me what there is in the bag, we don't know yet how much it contains. How much money there is in it might well make a difference as to what you can do next."

Caitlin reached into her plaid and handed the little bag over. Undoing the drawstring, Mary tipped the contents into the palm of her hand. There were just five silver shillings.

"Well, not a huge amount Caitlin. It hasn't made you a rich woman, but it's better than nothing.

SEBASTIAN DAVISON

Mary paused a moment as she considered what was the best way to help the girl...

"Here is what I'm going to do. Captain Larsson won't turn back or even change course for some little stowaway, so you are going to have to come with us to Liverpool anyway. "I'm going to talk to him and ask him to add you to the passenger list as part of my party, perhaps as my sister in law and try to persuade him not to report you to the authorities when we land. Though I'm afraid you will have to give him your money. And" she added, "in return, you can help me with these unruly children." Mary stroked the hair of her young son to show that she really loved them just the way they were.

Keeping Caitlin's five shillings in her hand, the older woman departed on her mission having told her children that they must stay with her new friend while she went and talked to the captain.

As Mary walked slowly along the deck towards the cabin at the stern of the ship, she offered up a small prayer for guidance, knowing full well that she was taking responsibility for a young life whose owner she had only just met. She realised that she could simply hand the stowaway over to Captain Larsson who would then in turn transfer her to the authorities once the ship had docked in Liverpool; but to do so was simply not in the good woman's nature. Without realising it she was relying on her in-built maternal instincts. At the doorway to the captain's cabin she took a deep breath then knocked firmly.

Left alone with the children, Caitlin felt a little bit more at ease. "After all," she thought, "they are younger than I and not so very different to any of the young friends and family I've left behind in the glen." But when she started to talk to them she found that she was struggling to understand what they were saying, nor could the children grasp much of what she said. What she didn't realise of course was that with an English father and Scottish mother they were speaking a mixture of English and Gaelic. It had

50

never occurred to her that anybody spoke in any other way than her native tongue. All the people she had ever met, including the Reverend and Mrs Bailey, had spoken the language of the Highlands of Scotland. Mary had spoken to the girl in Gaelic too, probably without thinking. However, having only recently left childhood herself, with the few words they had in common and by smiles, gestures and body language it was not too long before they could communicate quite well and the children were soon playing happily with their new found friend. Caitlin retrieved the little bundle of food that she had brought with her from the minister's house and the sharing of even the small amount of food there was made the process of getting to know each other so much easier.

About half an hour later, Mary Blake returned with the good news that the captain, after a great deal of persuasion had agreed to add Caitlin to the passenger list but had insisted that her fare must be paid. Mary had offered him the five shillings but when that was refused as insufficient, Mary had paid him another five on top of that out of her own pocket. She asked Caitlin to promise to pay her back as soon as she could as her own funds were extremely limited. Mary's generosity was entirely in keeping with her person- ality, believing as she did, that money and possessions should be shared with another if they had greater need and that a promise, once given, is a sacred thing that should never be broken. Caitlin agreed to this promise though she really had little choice, and as to how she was going to pay back the money she had no idea.

In fact she had very little knowledge of money at all. She knew what it was, but had never had cause to use it. She had known that her father had kept a few coins in a cloth bag that was kept under his mattress but the significance of their worth was completely lost on her. She had taken the shillings from the church knowing that they could be useful to her in some way but more as an act of defiance towards the vicious tyrant she was leaving behind.

Because of her isolated life in the glen and her captivity at the hands of Mrs Bailey in Oban, Caitlin's exposure to unfamiliar people was very limited, only rarely had they had visits from people living outside their own little community. Over the course of the three days that the voyage to Liverpool lasted, she became less nervous in the presence of strangers and with the security and comfort brought about by Mary's presence she learned to be more confident when one of the other five passengers or the crew spoke to her because all except one deckhand could speak Gaelic, so language was no barrier.

When Caitlin boarded the *Maid of Eriskay*, her only worldly possessions were the ragged clothes she was wearing, a few scraps of food and the five shilling pieces. Mary did have some clothes for herself and the children but due to her much, much larger size, she had nothing that would fit Caitlin. One of the other lady passengers who was travelling to Liverpool with them took pity on the tattered stowaway and gave her a warm, pale blue woollen dress that, with the help of a few stitches here and there was adjusted to fit her reasonably well. After a good scrub and with her hair washed and braided, Caitlin put on the new dress. New clothes and rosy cheeks immediately transformed the dirty, ragged child into a pretty and presentable young woman. She was undernourished from the miserable, inadequate rations that she had been given by Mrs Baillie but was otherwise fit and healthy.

Mary could see many similarities between Caitlin and herself as she had been in Fort William; simple and uncomplicated, living almost entirely in the present, a naïve and trusting country girl just as she herself had been a small-town fisherman's daughter, and as she grew to like and respect the young woman, she determined to try to give the girl the opportunities that she herself had not had but from which she would have benefited. Mary would probably still have been almost as uncomplicated as Caitlin, had it not been for her involvement with Henry Blake. The army and its strict regulations had been a huge surprise to her and it had taken her some considerable time and great goodwill and flexibility between husband and wife to come to terms with the huge differences there were between her upbringing, living her life around the sea, the storms and the tides, and the life of a soldier.

As the *Maid of Eriskay* slowly moved into one of the small docks on the banks of the Mersey, Caitlin, Mary and the two children stood by a portion of the rail that had not been damaged by the storm off Oban and gazed in amazement at the whole scene. None of them were prepared for this; the vast array of ships, warehouses and the seemingly frenetic and haphazard activity of a busy port. They had never seen such hustle and bustle, paved streets, hundreds of horses and carts, and huge numbers of people hurrying about their business. It was at the same time both exhilarating and terrifying. However, this was where they had to leave the relative security of the ship and head into the great unknown of the city itself.

They were to take lodgings with an acquaintance of Captain Larsson and he had arranged for a member of his crew, who was familiar with the layout of the streets of Liverpool to guide them and to carry their belongings. The house itself was part of a row of cottages not far from the docks, and although it was small and sparsely furnished, it was clean, with water to wash, good, though simple food and a bed of her own to sleep in. For the first few days, strange though it may seem, the comforts of civilisation made her feel slightly bewildered; being warm, dry, well-fed and comfortable all the time was so different to her life at home in the glen where existence could be harsh and living conditions primitive, But it didn't take long for her to begin to enjoy and appreciate these creature comforts.

When she recalled this time many years later, the most vivid memories that she had of her brief stay in such a huge city, were the smells; horse manure and sewers, pungent spices from the warehouses and the delicious aroma of cooking from the eating houses and taverns that were to be found in almost every street, especially those close to the waterfront.

It was here that Caitlin was first introduced to actually using money to buy something for herself. The two women, having left Angelina and Malcolm in the care of their kindly landlady, went in search of some new clothes for Caitlin. She still had only the woollen dress given to her by the other passenger on the *Maid of Eriskay*. As with women the world over, it didn't take Caitlin very long to begin to enjoy trying on new clothes and, with a little encouragement from the older and slightly more worldly-wise Mary, soon wanted to make the best of herself and to look as pretty as she could. And pretty she certainly was! Many were the admiring looks Caitlin got that day, though she was blithely oblivious to most of them.

Mary had paid for the clothes and they were returning home along the cobbled streets when they could smell the wonderful, mouth-watering aroma of fresh-baked bread coming from one of the many shops. Caitlin stopped and peeped in through the doorway, transfixed by the sight of row upon row of golden loaves on the shelves and the wonderful, mouth-watering smell. Mary rummaged in her purse and brought out three bright copper pennies.

"Go on, go in and buy some little bread rolls to take home for our dinner."

Caitlin hesitated, unsure of herself, but a little push was all it took and she bravely went into the shop on her own. After what seemed an eternity, the girl emerged, eyes bright with success, clutching several small, crisp, freshly baked loaves. Alas, not all the bread completed the journey to the boarding house, it was just too good and the two women walked contentedly homewards, nibbling fresh bread and chatting about their purchases. For Caitlin, the smell of baking bread would forever be associated with the streets of Liverpool.

Mary was becoming increasingly fond of her protégé, so much so that not long after they had arrived in Liverpool, with the assistance and guidance of Captain Larsson, whom she had come to trust and respect, she sold a little gold locket and chain that had been a present from her husband Henry. She was confident that he would have approved of her action, for he shared many of the same values and standards, particularly towards others. With the money so raised, Mary bought for Caitlin a ticket that would allow her to accompany them on the next step of their journey, the voyage across the ocean. Before doing so she asked Caitlin if this was what she wanted. Having finally found a friend and in that friend the love and support that she so desperately needed to allow her to feel that she was no longer alone in the world, Caitlin agreed immediately although in her ignorance she had absolutely no concept of what she was agreeing to. The vast expanses of the ocean with nothing but water and sailing out of sight of land for weeks on end had no meaning to her. The journey that she had already made from Oban to Liverpool was further than she could have ever dreamed possible, so to multiply that tenfold was beyond her wildest imagination.

There were so many dangers in such an alien environment as Liverpool and plenty of occasions when events could go seriously wrong for somebody as innocent and naive as Caitlin. On the first morning after they had disembarked, Caitlin was taking Angelina and Malcolm for a walk down towards the port, to allow Mary a few minutes of peace and to let the youngsters use up some of their pent-up energy, when, just as they were crossing one of the busy thoroughfares, she saw a fancy carriage pulled by four prancing grey horses galloping towards them, no doubt the transport of some important dignitary or one of the rich merchants. She could only stand and stare. She had never seen anything like it before in her life. Only at the last minute did the driver see the girl and two children standing motionless in his path. He shouted something unintelligible at them and swerved the horses. It was only the driver's skill and a good deal of luck that prevented a terrible accident.

A few days later, Caitlin was walking down one of the busy streets not far from their lodgings when she was accosted by a young and slightly drunk sailor who thought she was a street girl and therefore available. It was fortunate that Mary was there to interrupt the conversation and hurry a rather confused Caitlin away from the amorous sailor. The older woman then had to explain just what prostitution was and that she must be careful when talking to strange men. It was only when Mary pointed out some of the real street girls dressed as they were in cheap, very revealing clothes, with exaggerated make up and often slightly drunk as they stood on street corners plying their trade, that Caitlin realised just how close she had come to disaster. Had she been alone, she would probably have succumbed to the sailor's charms and as a consequence been drawn inexorably into the sordid and depraved underworld of this bustling and thriving city. As a seaport, Liverpool was no different to any other anywhere in the world where ignorant or innocent people could be destroyed by those whose motives were greed or gratification. As the days went by Mary was delighted to see that her friend was becoming much less intimidated by the strangeness of city life and was talking and smiling much more than she had at first as she became more familiar with the people and places around her. When Mary watched Caitlin and the children at play, it seemed as if they had known each other all their lives.

One evening, the two women were sitting quietly before the fire in their lodgings. They had not yet bothered to light the small oil lamp that was the room's only illumination, content rather to enjoy the last of the daylight and the soft, glowing fire. Revelling in the peace and tranquillity of the time after the children had gone to sleep and before they retired themselves; in a time of reflection and consideration of things gone by; a thought came to Mary. 'It seems strange that Caitlin never talks about her mother. I wonder why that is?' She decided to broach the subject.

"My Dear, I know that we haven't been together for very long, but I have never heard you mention your mother. Do you just not like her? Or has something happened to her? You don't have to tell me if it upsets you at all."

Caitlin was silent and pensive for a minute; she sat quietly, with her hands folded on the lap of her new skirt, gazing deep into the little flames as they flickered in the grate. Then with a gentle sigh she replied.

"Oh no, I'm not unhappy about it. In fact, I can hardly remember my mother at all. She died when I was no more than a young child. My Father once told me that she had been ill for a long time and before the end, she was coughing up blood. So I think it must have been a sickness of her lungs that killed her. All I am really mindful of is the way her dress seemed to smell. Sometimes it was a peaty smoky smell and at other times it was of cooking. There was also another funny, oily smell. I learned after she died that it was the smell of the wool that she had been preparing for spinning. We didn't have many sheep and my mother did all the spinning for everybody in the glen. My Aunt Flora looked after me when I was little and taught me the things that my father couldn't."

Mary reached across and touched the younger woman's hand.

"I'm sorry my dear. I will try to teach you the things you need to know. If I know it myself." She added with a chuckle.

The ship that was to take them on the Atlantic crossing was the three-masted barque *Andromeda*; a nearly new vessel, well suited and prepared for ocean crossing, though even a ship, sturdily built by one of the finest shipyards in England as she was, would be tested on a voyage across the Atlantic as late in the year as this. She was one of the few vessels that had been built in the Royal Naval Dockyard in Portsmouth that was not actually a warship. The intention had been that she should be used to carry supplies to the various naval depots around the world - South Africa and

India in particular -but almost as soon as she was completed, the Admiralty decided that it was cheaper to put this work out to tender by civilian companies. Consequently *Andromeda* was sold out of naval service almost as soon as she left the slipway. Because of her origins, she had been built to a much higher standard than ordinary commercial vessels of that time and as a consequence was very well suited to the North Atlantic trade routes. When it came to restocking their overseas bases, speed and reliability were considered to be of lesser importance by the Royal Navy than the cost of the supplies themselves.

The *Andromeda* should have set sail some time before this, but due to the late arrival in Liverpool of a large portion of her cargo; a consignment of cannons, musket balls and a considerable quantity of gunpowder from the Woolwich Arsenal munitions factory in London, her departure had been postponed several times. It was never determined what caused the delay, but the delivery of these items of ordnance was deemed vital to the success of the British forces in Canada; so as Andromeda was the last scheduled crossing of the ocean to be made before winter, and her owners had a large supply contract with the Navy to deliver goods all over the world, it would have been unthinkable to have sailed without them.

Every morning, leaving the children behind at the lodgings in the care of their kindly landlady, the two women went down to the dockside office of the shipping line to enquire when *Andromeda* would sail. Every morning the cheeky young clerk behind the desk would give them the same answer.

"We're still waiting for the arrival of a very special cargo; you had better call again tomorrow."

Finally after just over two weeks, by which time they were beginning to give up hope of ever leaving England and Mary was beginning to worry that her meagre funds would run out before they sailed, the clerk told them;

"The special cargo came in on the tide last night and has got to be trans-shipped out in the river. The dockyard owners won't allow all that gunpowder into the dock. So they've moved the ship out and she's now at anchor in mid-stream. She's been there since this morning and they'll want to leave on the top of the tide this afternoon. If you want to sail on her you'll have to be quick and get someone with a little boat to take you out there. You'll have to look sharp though," The clerk looked up at the large clock on the office wall. "High Water's at three o'clock and it's nearly twelve-fifteen now."

"We will have to go and fetch the children and our bags first," said Mary. "Do you know of a boatman who will take us?"

"That I do. My brother Tom will take you, but he'll charge you a shilling."

"I'm in no position to haggle," grumbled Mary. "Though I think its daylight robbery. Tell your brother to be ready as soon as possible and we will go and collect our things and return here just as quickly as we can."

Within the hour, an hour of absolute confusion, the two women had returned to their lodgings, packed up what few belongings they had and handed over some more of Mary's ever-dwindling savings in payment to the startled and disappointed landlady who had been expecting her guests to stay a while longer. Just in time, they presented themselves together with the two bewildered children back at the offices of the shipping line where they were bundled into Tom's tiny rowing boat. Within only a few minutes, the whole family were being thoroughly soaked by the muddy, salty water of the Mersey as they were taken out to the *Andromeda*. Malcolm, as any small boy might, thought it was all very funny but the others were not so happy. The ship was a wonderful sight, with all her sails furled loosely to her yards, but otherwise ready and eager to be on her way as soon as the loading of her cargo was completed.

The whole trip out to the ship was completed in about half an hour, but it was four cold, wet passengers that embarked for their passage to the New World.

As soon as the precious munitions, for which she had waited so long, were safely stowed away the good ship *Andromeda* weighed anchor from the river Mersey and left British shores bound for St John's, Newfoundland, the nearest port on the eastern side of the American continent, a distance of just over two thousand miles. Not the longest of voyages but one that had little protection or safe havens from the terrible Atlantic storms that could sweep across the ocean at any time of year. Leaving as they were, at the beginning of October, at the time of the autumn equinox, gale force winds and raging seas were almost a certainty.

Deep in the hold, along with the explosives was a vast array of goods that were essential to life in the New World; items that could not be obtained from the sea, or the forests and rivers of a newly settled country. There were shovels and axes for the farmers and woodsmen, rolls of cloth and sewing needles for the sailmakers and housewives, bars of iron for the blacksmiths to convert into horseshoes, cart axles and anything and everything that was needed by any busy port. On board, as well as Mary, Caitlin and the two children, were several other families who were taking the same great leap of faith by journeying across two thousand miles of stormy ocean to a new life in an unknown land.

CHAPTER SEVEN

They had hardly left the shelter of Liverpool Bay when the first storm of the voyage started to blow in earnest. The confused waves of the Irish Sea seemed to make *Andromeda*, stout vessel though she was, roll uncomfortably in several different directions at the same time. In other gales later in the voyage, the waves would be much larger and the wind much stronger, but the motion of the ship in the deep ocean appeared to be far more regular. All this erratic movement caused many of the passengers and even some of the crew to be violently seasick. Although they knew that they would recover in a day or so, the knowledge did little to lessen the misery of the sufferers. Caitlin, Angelina and Malcolm however were some of the lucky ones not to be affected. Surprisingly, considering that she had been afloat in some of the roughest waters of the Western Isles of Scotland for most of her adult life, Mary was laid low. This was probably because the motion of the much larger *Andromeda* was very different, slow and rhythmical whereas the little fishing boats would have seemed to bounce over the waves. Whatever the actual cause, it was Caitlin who had to look after the children's needs for almost a week until their mother recovered her strength and her appetite.

Life on board ship seemed to suit Caitlin and although after the first ten days or so all the fresh food had either been eaten or gone rotten, she could and did eat everything that was put before her, even the salt beef and hard ship's biscuits. On a comparatively short voyage such as this, there was no need to ration the passengers and the plentiful supply of nourishment, together with the sea air and the absence of the gruelling hard work, helped put back much of the weight and vigour that she had lost during her months of drudgery and near starvation with the Baillies in Oban.

Sailing north-west across the Irish Sea, the Isle of Man was passed to starboard, though not seen because of the poor visibility in the gale. On through St George's Channel, past Rathlin Island, the northern Irish coast soon disappeared, and with it the dangers that are associated with coastal waters. *Andromeda* hurried swiftly out into the great waters of the North Atlantic as if eager to begin the main part of her journey.

After a few days out on the open ocean and with the worst of the seasickness behind them, the travellers began to settle into a routine. The passengers knew that they had a voyage of around four weeks ahead of them, although this would be very dependent on the weather that they encountered during the voyage. There was no work expected of them so there was plenty of time to become used to the slower pace of life on-board.

Although the long voyage on a crowded ship could have become somewhat monotonous, there were just enough interesting moments to liven up their days at sea. During one particular spell of fine weather with breeze enough to fill the enormous sails but insufficient to send the passengers hurrying below deck to stay dry and warm, a large pod of huge whales, which the knowledgeable sailors told them were humpback whales, accompanied them for several hours, much to the excitement and amusement of the children who never tired of watching the waves, waiting for the huge animals to resurface, greeting each spurt of vapour with shouts of 'Thar she bloows'. When a particularly large male surfaced close to the ship and as the animal was directly upwind of them it was discovered that humans were not the only animals that could have bad breath! All too soon these amazing creatures departed to continue on their journey that would have no end, leaving the ship alone among the rolling waves.

Long after the whales had disappeared, Caitlin lingered on deck tucked into a sheltered corner beside the mainmast. She rather hoped that the enormous creatures would reappear, but was not really too bothered whether they did or not, just content to sit quietly in the sunshine and spend a little while on her own, so she was rather surprised when she heard herself addressed in her own native tongue.

"Good day, missy. May I sit with you awhile?"

She turned to see who was speaking and was somewhat surprised to see the Second Mate standing beside her. With a nod of acquiescence, she moved along the narrow bench on which she was sitting to make room for the newcomer. Not quite sure of what to do or say, she remained silent and waited for him to speak again. The greying hair tied with tarry yarn into a little queue, the straggling beard and brown, weather-beaten face showed her a man who had been at sea for many years.

"I venture to approach you, because 'tis good to hear my own tongue spoken again. English speaking is all very fine, I daresay, but I like far better the speech I learned at my mother's knee. Whereabouts do you hail from if I may be so bold?"

As far as Caitlin was aware, her birthplace had no name, so she could only think to mention a place nearby that she knew.

"My home was not too far from Glencoe, sir. In a little glen called Etive."

"A bonny place to be sure my dear. But not too safe in these troubled times. Were you driven from your home as so many others have been?"

63

"Others of my family were, but I was away up the hillside when it happened, so I avoided the soldiers. Though," she added. "my existence was destroyed as surely as if I had been at home. Were you driven away too?"

"Not really, I was already at sea when my father's land was "required" by those dammed invaders. And I don't mean the sheep, rather the Sassenach usurpers who have no care for the likes of you and me." He replied bitterly. "And what good is my island for the grazing of sheep other than those that can live upon the kelp from the seashore. I am from the main island of Orkney." He finished by way of explanation.

"Are they Sassenach sheep?" Caitlin asked innocently.

The second mate laughed.

"No, no, my dear. The sheep themselves are as Scottish as ourselves, but they are being put to graze on the land that has been taken from us and our families by the greedy and rich lords from England so that they can become even richer."

"Why do we not just take our homes back?"

"A few have tried, but all they gained was a quick death and a lonely grave. The time will come maybe when all will be well again, but until that day dawns, we must wait and remember the ways of our homes and our relatives. The waiting may well be long and generations may have to pass before we regain what is rightfully ours and redress the bloodshed."

"One day I will put right the wrongs that my family have suffered."

"Amen to that my dear. Keep that hope in your heart and you will have done all that you can to keep alive the hopes and dreams of many a broken Highlander."

Suddenly, in a moment of impulse and emotion, the old sailor grasped Caitlin's hand and raising it to his lips, kissed her fingers gently, then turned and walked quickly away across the rolling deck.

Caitlin sat quietly for a time, trying to understand what the old man had meant. But she was a girl of the glens and had no idea of politics or power struggles. She had had no formal education and the only influences from the world outside the glen had been the slightly confused Bible stories told to her by her uncle Iain who had fancied himself as something of a preacher though his ministry had not been recognised by the elders of any kirk. She went in search of Mary.

Although Mary was older and had had some exposure to the happenings of the outside world, largely through the eyes of her husband, she was still uncertain of the reasons behind all the violence that had been going on and tried to explain why so many people were being evicted from their houses and land as best she could, and, in an effort to comfort and reassure the younger woman, she finished by saying; "After all, we're leaving all these horrible and bloody things behind us now and I'm sure we'll have enough problems to concern us when we arrive in Newfoundland."

This seemed to satisfy Caitlin's young and uncomplicated mind and although she felt somewhat subdued for the rest of that day, by the following morning, she was back to her normal, cheerful self.

Soon after the halfway point of the voyage and about as far from land and protection as they would ever be, the sails of another ship were sighted on the horizon. Their shape and the set of the rigging soon caused the captain to become suspicious and as the courses of the vessels converged, his suspicions turned to alarm. The other ship was identified as a French Man-o-War which would have been only too delighted to capture them; not only for the prize money that the crew would obtain from the sale of such a prize, but also to deny so many vital supplies that they were carrying to the soldiers of the country with which they, the French were at war. However, much to the relief of all aboard the *Andromeda*, when the other vessel was sighted, their own ship was a long way to windward and with night approaching there was little hope of a close encounter. The French vessel was sailing eastwards, on her way back home, probably after several years abroad, and as a consequence, with no proper facilities for beaching and cleaning in Northern America, her hull would have been covered in weeds and barnacles, slowing her down even further. For these reasons, or perhaps because she was in a hurry to complete her crossing, she continued on her course making no attempt to intercept the *Andromeda*. The captain of the *Andromeda* however took the precaution of altering course as soon as darkness fell and headed due north and away from the course of the "Frenchman" as fast as the ship would sail. When daylight showed no sign of the other vessel, he was confident that there was no further danger and he resumed his westerly course. However, just in case the same thing happened again, he gave orders that lookouts were to be posted around the clock.

Towards the end of the passage, as they crossed the area of shallow water known as the Grand Banks, a thick, dense, blinding fog settled over the ship, and for three days their world reached no further than the rails of the deck. Even the mastheads disappeared, and though these murky conditions are usually associated with calm weather, the sails were still filled with wind, and they continued to rush madly onward with no way of knowing what was ahead. They could only have blind faith in the ship's compass and pray that no other ship was close by. Icebergs had been seen in this area on previous voyages but these were a spring and early summer phenomenon and by this late in the year, all would have been melted away by the warmer seas of summer. They encountered nothing that caused concern but even so it was with great relief when they sailed clear of the blanketing fog with no misfortunes.

Despite the boredom and cramped conditions, Angelina and Malcolm behaved impeccably, due in no small part to Caitlin who worked very hard to maintain harmony among the family and all the other passengers. She was still young enough to giggle at silly childish things but mature enough to know when to calm things down. She was so grateful to Mary for her help that she would have done anything she could to be of use and during this voyage developed a bond with the woman who had really taken over the role of mother, a bond that would last the rest of her life. For it was Mary who was helping her to make the transition from a simple country girl to a confidant, competent woman who could survive in the big wide world into which she had been thrown.

Mary in her turn was very glad of Caitlin's company and companionship so the gratitude was not entirely one-way. She had not been looking forward to the voyage very much. Not only because of the difficulties of taking two small children almost half-way across the world on her own but also because she had serious doubts as to whether she would be able to cope with the change of lifestyle that she knew awaited her in Newfoundland. In Fort William she was a part of the community and free to do almost anything she wished. In her eyes, she was a woman as good as any man in a male dominated society, but when she arrived in St John's, she would simply be the wife of another officer in the Marines. She felt she was too ignorant of the protocols that would be expected of her in that role and would be an embarrassment to her husband. She should not have worried however, from the moment they arrived, whatever she lacked in knowledge and education was far outweighed by the effect her amazing personality would have on the other military women; and their husbands too! Her 'enormous' personality, and mass of red hair, her twinkling blue eyes and ready smile worked wonders, winning the hearts of all those who met her.

So there was relief for all on board when *Andromeda* sailed into the port of St John's on the island of Newfoundland after a passage of twenty nine days. No illness or injuries had occurred and the entire cargo was intact and dry; in all a satisfactory and uneventful voyage, but an unforgettable adventure for all her passengers; most of whom would never put to sea again.

CHAPTER EIGHT

The entrance to the harbour of St John's is fairly constricted, though the depth of water is more than sufficient for the safe entry of any ship whatever the state of the tide. Having passed through this restricted channel, an inbound vessel would then have to turn almost ninety degrees to the left, or port in nautical terms, and could then moor quite safely to the quayside or to one of the small jetties that had been built at the furthest end of this magnificent haven, safe from the wind and waves whatever direction they may come from. High above the Narrows, as this narrow strip of water is appropriately called, stands Signal Hill, where a lookout would, no doubt have been searching the horizon throughout daylight hours whenever a ship was expected, and would have sent word to the garrison and to the Harbourmaster. The news would spread like wildfire and there would be plenty of time for the townspeople to come down to the waterfront to watch as a new ship, full of essential cargo and more importantly, letters from England and fresh news of their loved ones who now seemed so far away.

As they stood at the ship's rail waiting impatiently for the mooring lines to be secured, Mary and the children eagerly scanned the crowded dockside trying to pick out the familiar face of Henry Blake. Although they had not seen their father for about eighteen months, Angelina and Malcolm were both old enough to remember what he looked like, and were so disappointed when his face was nowhere to be seen. Tears fell as the two women did their best to comfort them whist fighting back their own disappointment.

Most of the other passengers had disembarked and the crew and dock workers were beginning to open the holds ready to start unloading the cargo when a young man who was unfamiliar to the older woman but was wearing a soldier's uniform with the insignia of Henry Blake's regiment climbed the gangway. He walked carefully across the cluttered deck and approached Mary.

"Mrs Blake? Your husband sends his apologies and regrets that he cannot be here to greet you today, but he was ordered to sea some four days ago because we received reports that there were some French ships in these waters. Before he left, he detailed me to meet you and escort you and your belongings back to the garrison. I have a handcart down on the wharf for them. The lieutenant told me that he hopes to return within a week or so." He paused and with a cheeky grin, swept off his cap, bowed low, and smiled.

"Now that I have delivered my official military message, may I be the first to welcome you to St John's. "And the children too". He added hastily.

In a voice, which she hoped carried some sort of authority, as befitted the wife of an officer and having noted the man's rank from the insignia on his shoulder Mary replied;

"Thank you Corporal. Our bags, few as they are, have already been brought on deck and are ready beside the gangway for your immediate attention."

Indicating Caitlin standing beside her wearing her best dress, which she thought was appropriate to her arrival onto a new continent, her golden hair gleaming in the late autumn sunshine, Mary added. "This is Miss Munroe who joined us in Liverpool and will be staying with us for the time being as one of the family."

Suitably chastened by these remarks, the soldier hurriedly replaced his cap and replied crisply.

"Yes ma'am. Straightaway ma'am." Then turned and went about his errand. But as he went, he gave Caitlin a friendly wink.

A soon as all the bags had been checked and carried off the ship, Mary, Caitlin, Angelina and Malcolm descended the gangplank and set foot on the soil of Newfoundland for the very first time, and although they were all grateful to the sturdy ship *Andromeda*, her captain and her crew for bringing them safely across so many miles of ocean, none of them gave so much as a backward glance as they left the dockside, looking towards the future with a mixture of excitement, and trepidation as they embarked on the final step of their journey into the unknown.

Though less than two months had passed since the children had discovered her hiding in the little ship off Oban, Caitlin had become an almost indispensable part of the family, and so it was automatically assumed that she would move into the lieutenant's quarters in the garrison along with Mary and the children. No alternatives had even been considered. Mary had a lot of explaining to do when her husband returned from sea a few days later, to find that there was an additional member of the family, but Henry Blake was a tolerant man and liked Caitlin from the outset. He straightaway understood that she had nowhere else to go. He realised that to turn her out onto the streets, innocent and unworldly as she was, would be contrary to the principles to which both he and Mary adhered. Though she had learned so much since leaving Glen Etive she was still far from ready to live on her own with no experienced hand to guide and help her. When Mary told him of the sale of the gold locket and chain to pay for Caitlin's fare, Henry told his wife she had made the right decision and that he would have done exactly the same himself. He was pleased that his wife had found a friend to help replace those she had left behind in

Fort William, so accepted the newcomer to his family with genuine goodwill and courtesy.

The lieutenant's quarters inside the high stone walls of the garrison were hardly luxurious. Impersonal and austere described them best. Although they were originally intended as living quarters for middle-ranking unaccompanied male officers, with the number of soldiers stationed there having been reduced in recent times, Henry Blake had been able to obtain permission for his family to move into the garrison as others had done recently.

Situated beside a raised walkway that encircled the open expanse of the parade ground, the accommodation comprised of a single large main room with two small bedrooms leading off it and a little roofed porch at the rear which served as a storage, washing and play area. Henry had lived alone in these rooms for almost a year, his domestic needs catered for by a native servant, and although the place was relatively clean, it lacked the cosy feel that only a woman can provide. Mary and Caitlin soon began to put homely touches to their new quarters and convert a set of spartan barrack rooms into a dwelling fit for a family. A curtain here, a cushion there, a vase of dried grasses in the window was all it took; the addition of the chatter of children and some appetizing smells and the transformation was almost miraculous. Caitlin had to share a room with the two children but was able to hang a bed sheet by way of a curtain to screen off her bed and allow her some privacy whenever she felt the need.

As is the way of young children, when presented with completely new surroundings, Angelina and Malcolm soon learnt their way around the garrison and where they could and could not go. They were quite content to stay nearby so that if they were unsure of themselves or nervous about anything they could check that their mother or Caitlin was not too far away. Henry was delighted to have his wife and children close to him again and once the slight nervousness caused by having a "father figure" in the family again had faded away, the children liked nothing better than to play soldiers with him and many a time, they could be seen being marched round the parade ground in games of mock "drill".

Compared to European cities, St John's was not a large place, though it was one of the most important in the north of the New World. Situated as it was on the east coast of the large island of Newfoundland, just off the eastern coast of Canada, it was a landfall town for ships from across the ocean and was the first safe haven where they could replenish their dwindling supplies of wood and water if required or make any repairs that might be necessary before continuing their voyage up the mighty St Lawrence River to Quebec and Montreal another thousand miles or so deep into the continent. The massive stone breakwater allowed greater protection to ships moored to the wooden jetties that had been built out into the water so that even the largest vessels could remain afloat whatever the state of the tide. The waterfront was lined with warehouses to store both incoming and outgoing cargoes. There were repair yards with blacksmiths' forges, sailmakers lofts and carpenters shops, net makers and yards for the builders of small boats. Scattered among these commercial premises were taverns and ale houses where the proprietors, and some of the locals, whilst providing a cordial atmosphere and expensive beer, did their best to relieve the unsuspecting and often inebriated sailors of their hard earned pay by any means they could before they left town to return to sea once more.

In addition to catering for the transatlantic trade, St John's was also one of the major centres of the Grand Banks cod fishery where much of the fish caught would be split, dried and salted before being put into wooden barrels for export to Europe; a useful and lucrative return cargo for many of the merchant ships, such as *Andromeda*, that helped make great fortunes for many of the vessels' owners.

In fine weather, every available space around the dockside would be covered with racks of drying codfish. Not the best place to be for anybody with a delicate sense of smell!

The buildings that lined the quayside and the waterfront were, for the most part, huge warehouses several stories high and built almost entirely of locally sourced wood. The gable ends were fitted with strong lifting gantries extending out over the wharf that could lift goods to upper floors where cargoes were accumulated for loading or the materials discharged from the incoming vessels could be stored before distribution. There was insufficient room for all the necessary buildings in just one row, so, in the side streets at right angles to the main waterfront and on another street, slightly up the hillside, away from the water but running parallel to the waterfront were the ship's chandlers and trading posts. It was here that the residents of the town and its visitors could purchase an amazing selection of wares for their own and business use.

In fact it was rather like a maritime frontier town with a population to match. Most nationalities, colours and creeds were there, people running away from a past life, others looking for a better life in the new world. Perhaps not too surprisingly, there weren't very many older people. As in many other pioneering towns and cities life expectancy was not very high; hard work, poor or unbalanced nutrition and a profound lack of medical assistance made the sight of a very old man or woman something of a rarity. Life was hard, but no more so than in most other new settlements throughout North America.

For the most part food was plentiful. Fish formed a large part of the diet; with the Grand Banks not far away out to sea, great catches of cod were caught and landed in St John's. Venison and other game were often brought to the town to be traded for supplies by the trappers and the native inhabitants. Even beaver meat was sometimes eaten though its taste left something to be desired and consequently was not universally popular. Bread was expensive because most of the flour had to be imported either from Europe or further south, along the coast of the mainland where the climate was mild enough for the production of wheat and maize. Small quantities of barley and oats were grown locally by farmers having cleared some of the scrub land with great difficulty and many months of back-breaking toil. Potatoes and turnips were planted wherever the soil was sufficiently rich and seemed to thrive well enough in these climatic conditions and provided a most welcome variety to an otherwise somewhat monotonous diet. With a large proportion of the population being Irish or of Irish descent, the humble potato was always in great demand.

Shortly after the arrival of Mary, Caitlin and the children in St John's, winter began in earnest; not great quantities of snow and ice, but cold, cold rain and bitter winds blowing from the arctic seas to the north; or damp and chilling fogs that could last for days, enveloping the entire city with a gloomy and impenetrable blanket. But along with all the other residents new and old, they endured and they survived.

Christmas, long awaited by the children was celebrated in the company of the other residents of the garrison, and the Blake family were made welcome into several households in the town, espe-cially those families who had members working in the garrison as civilians or those who were able to trade with the militia to supply food, fuel and other local produce. The little church of St John was gaily decorated with pine branches and many candles were lit to brighten the gloom of that midwinter day. Hymns and carols were sung, people dressed in their best clothes and a huge traditional Christmas meal was enjoyed. It was a day of peace and goodwill, and a celebration of all the traditions that had been brought by the different nationalities from whichever European country they had originated.

CHAPTER NINE

As soon as the festivities of Christmas and the New Year were over, mindful of the money Mary had spent on her behalf; especially her transatlantic fare as well as the 'incentive' that had had to be paid to the captain of the *Maid of Eriskay* not to expose her as a stowaway, and for her lodgings in Liverpool, Caitlin began to search for employment and within a few days discovered that an assistant was required at the largest of the trading post stores on Water Street, the busy thoroughfare just up the hill from the waterfront. Intermingled with the trader's premises and warehouses were department stores where you could purchase almost any item that you might need; gaily coloured ribbons and pretty dresses, snowshoes and animal traps, guns and tobacco, bacon and dried beans.

The idea of having to serve the store customers all day filled Caitlin with all sorts of fears and misgivings. Her confidence was improving day by day but she was still rather diffident when talking to complete strangers. When Henry tried to explain what employment actually was; that a job was working for somebody else with payment of money in return, all Caitlin could think of was her dreadful experience with Mrs Baillie. He reassured her that working in a trading store would be very different to the situation in Oban. He told her that the time she had spent there had been tantamount to slavery and that he and Mary would be there to make certain that she was not exploited again. After a huge amount of encouragement from both Mary and Henry and determined as she was to repay her debts, she agreed to go to see the proprietor and discover whether the job was something she could do; but only if Mary would go with her to give her some support. Her friend willingly agreed with this because she was fairly sure that if Caitlin had to attend the interview on her own, her nerves would fail her and she would never actually get there at all.

The largest and most popular store, and the one that was trying to recruit new staff, was owned by a man called David Harrison, who had become, by nature of his prosperity and fair trading, a popular and respected resident of St John's. A native of Bristol who had arrived in the port about ten years previously, he had been intent on making his living as a trader. He had reasoned rather perceptively, that in a new country, whether people made a fortune or lost everything they possessed, if they were a farmer or a fisherman, a sailor or a trapper, local inhabitant or newly arrived from overseas, they all, without exception, needed food and clothing which together with all the other necessities of life he would be in an excellent position to provide. Whilst providing all these needs, he could make a good and potentially profitable living in the process without taking many of the risks and uncertainties that were inevitable in the other available occupations. By a combination of hard work, considerable business acumen and a reputation for fair trading, sadly an attribute not to be found in quite a few other establishments, David's store had become one of the most successful establishments on Water Street.

His father had been a grocer in Bristol, a well-established seaport in the south-west of England and David had spent many hours playing and then working in the shop from being quite a small boy. He had studied hard and learned the trade diligently, expecting to follow in his father's footsteps and take over the business when his parents were ready to retire. But in a rash rebellious moment, and much to his family's dismay, when only eighteen and in search of a life with more excitement than counting biscuits or weighing up bags of flour he had signed on as a deckhand on a whaling ship, the *Hecate* that was visiting the port. His idealistic and romantic notions of a more exciting life chasing the greatest creatures on earth however were soon brought to an abrupt end. The privations and brutally hard work on board a whaler during a long and bitter arctic winter were a cruel awakening to him and he knew that this life at sea was not for him. Three of his fellow crewmen were lost overboard from the *Hecate* or drowned when their fragile hunting boats were smashed during fights with wounded whales, and several others were either injured or disabled by frostbite. He was so totally disenchanted by the dangers and the uncivilised habits of many of the whaler men that he had jumped ship in St John's and determined to try his luck as a trader in the town. He was fortunate that the time was just right for the development of a chandlery.

David was well aware that he had caused great anguish and distress to his family by running away to sea, but he was confident that his father would be pleased that he wanted to make good use of the training and experience that he had gained whilst working in the shop in Bristol; albeit in a town far away. So he had plucked up courage and written to his father and asked him to back him in his new venture. Rather than send him money, he requested that he send him the goods and provisions with which to open a small shop. He had enclosed a list of the things that he thought might sell well in an up and coming harbour, things that he knew had been profitable back in the busy port of Bristol, where shipping and the docks had been a sizeable part of the shop's business. His father had agreed to his request though had written a letter to his son expressing great sadness that he would not be returning home and carrying on the family business as had been originally planned. Over the next few years whilst the chandlery business was in its infancy, his father's experience in the trade had been invaluable as he had many contacts and although father and son never met again, they gradually re-established a friendship, by letter and by trade across the Atlantic that became much closer as the years went on and that continued right up until the older man's death many years later.

At the time arranged for the interview, Caitlin and Mary entered the store and were invited into David's office at the back of the shop. It was only a small room without really enough room for the furniture that was already in it; a large desk, a chair and several shelves lined with the ledgers and files for the running of the shop; not to mention two coils of rope and a large sack of dried beans. When two more chairs were added to accommodate the two women, little room was left for the proprietor himself.

As first meetings go, it was something of a disaster because Caitlin was completely overcome with shyness and the formality of the occasion. Whenever David asked her a question, rather than answer herself, the girl would just stare at her own feet, and then look imploringly across at Mary, begging her to answer the question for her. But she need not have worried; David was charming and courteous by nature and with considerable patience and a lot of help from Mary, he was able to put Caitlin sufficiently at ease to extract enough information to clearly see that she could be of some use to him in the store.

Starting work in the store marked another great step in Caitlin's life. For the first time she was stepping out on her own, out from under the protective wing of Mary Blake and her family that had covered and protected her ever since she had left Oban. Without this shelter her situation would have been perilous indeed but it was time to leave her little cocoon and begin her life as an independent person. It was indeed a momentous moment on that first morning as she left the garrison looking very nervous and vulnerable to walk down the hill to the store. Frightened and fearful of the unknown tasks that lay before her as she was, Caitlin was also very determined to do whatever she had to do to repay the money that she owed. Mary watched her go from the little porch behind their lodging, filled with pride at what she had achieved in Caitlin's development; but also with a tinge of sadness that perhaps she was no longer needed.

When Caitlin started working at Harrison's store, as the youngest and most junior member of staff, her duties were very menial and uncomplicated, cleaning and sweeping, fetching and carrying anything and everything to and from the warehouse and the shop. She was kept busy from the moment the store opened till long after it closed at night, so it was something of a surprise to David, when, during a slack moment only a few weeks after starting at the chandlery, he came out of his office into the store and noticed her wandering among the goods that lay in piles around the room, touching and feeling some of the items for sale, her fingers running over sacks of flour, horses' harness, shovels. It wasn't until he saw her walking her fingers up a stack of rolls of cloth, then up another one that he realised that she was actually making a mental list of the items they had in stock. Just to prove to himself what he had seen, having surreptitiously counted them himself, he later asked the girl how many bags of musket balls they had in stock. When she immediately replied with the correct number he realised that he had an assistant who would become invaluable to him and to the store.

How right he was. As she overcame her initial shyness, Caitlin proved to be more and more useful to him. Soon she was spending much of her time looking after the needs and requirements of the customers rather than just the mundane, though equally essential work in the storerooms behind the chandlery.

Caitlin continued to live with the Blake family, returning home every evening to the garrison, weary but content, to a warm welcome and squeals of delight from the children. She still assisted Mary by helping to look after the children in the evenings and also as her companion and confidante when the lieutenant was at sea; which he frequently was. Every Sunday morning, would see her taking Angelina and Malcolm to the little Scottish church up on the hillside and, if the weather was fine enough the three of them would walk along the harbour side, sometimes even as far as the foot of Signal Hill that overlooked the Narrows at the entrance to the harbour. By taking charge of the children for a few hours like this Mary was able to have a little time to herself to do whatever she pleased; catch up on any neglected household chores, or as was more often the case, just to put her feet up and have an uninterrupted nap.

The garrison was continually bustling with military life, with all the comings and goings of the soldiers, with orders being shouted and the tramp of many feet, but it was a lonely, impersonal place and although there were a few other women living within the walls, Caitlin's presence as a familiar, friendly face and someone to talk to every day was of great comfort to Mary. Despite putting a brave face on things, she had found it difficult to adapt to the change of lifestyle that her move to St John's had forced upon her. She was still feeling very homesick for the freedom that her own little fishing boat had given her as well as the old friends and faces in the fishing community that she had left behind. The loneliness was made more acute by the fact that every one of the other soldiers' wives who were living in the garrison at that time was from south of the border in England and only able to speak to the newcomers in English. So it was comforting to both Caitlin and Mary to have each other and to be able to converse in Gaelic, the language they both still felt most comfortable speaking. As time went on both of them became fluent in English, though neither of them, Mary in particular, ever lost the strong accent of their homeland.

During the long dark, cold evenings and nights of winter the older woman taught her friend how to read and write, skills which Caitlin had never needed in the glen, but she now realised that her life could go no further without. It was not long before she became quite adept at both of these and would avidly read anything and everything that she could find, referring to Mary or Henry when she came across anything she didn't understand. Many were the nights when Mary would go into the room where Caitlin slept with the children to say goodnight only to find her young friend fast asleep with a book still clasped in her hand and the candle still burning in the little candlestick. Arithmetic she found a different matter; this was much more difficult to grasp. She could count very quickly and could remember quantities with ease but adding one strange symbol to another and making a third just did not make sense. It wasn't till Mary produced a small pile of pennies and used them to show just how numerical symbols could actually relate to real things that Caitlin began to comprehend the beginnings of mathematics. Realizing their importance however she persevered and with Mary's patient tuition learned the basics which she could develop further as time went on.

Languages however gave her no problems; and having sorted out, with relative ease the mixture of Gaelic and English that, Angelina and Malcolm had spoken when first they met, she began to develop an ability to understand and communicate with most of the people who came into the store regardless of the tongue they spoke. She was a natural with the spoken word. There were plenty of different tongues for her to get to grips with; sailors and settlers from all over the world passed through St John's and a fair proportion of them came to purchase their many and diverse needs from the huge range of goods that Harrison's store could offer. A Swede might want some tobacco or a German some trousers, but they were all most surprised when their store assistant was an attractive young woman who could actually converse, at least to some degree, with them in their own tongue, simple phrases at first but even that improved as time went on. Before long, even some of the strange dialects spoken by the local tribes made sense to her, though to most other people they did not.

Many of these indigenous North American languages did not possess any real written form. The few records they had were just a series of simple but descriptive pictures that had been inscribed on carefully prepared birch bark. But as many of these peoples were partially or completely nomadic, books, pictures or anything actually written down would have been, quite literally a burden to them. Instead, the tribal histories were retained by word of mouth; stories told and handed down from generation to generation. These people had prodigious memories and many stories were told in the form of accurately remembered songs or chants that could often last for hours on end.

Over the next two years, Caitlin's life began to settle down into a routine. Working in the store, helping Mary and doing her best to comprehend the complexities of grammar and mathematics left her little time for relaxation. The seasons came and went; she watched as the children grew and flourished and as she developed her skills in reading and writing she became more and more useful to her employer. Those around her watched as she matured into a composed, beautiful and increasingly competent young woman.

David came to trust her implicitly and began to ask her opinion about all sorts of practical matters in the store, especially about which goods they should stock that would be most likely to appeal to women and to the native people that came to them to make their purchases. Her fluency in languages helped enormously in being able to discover exactly what the customers wanted to buy rather than the store trying to guess what was best to sell. Perhaps a braided rope was more suited for hunting than a twisted one; high topped boots without holes for laces kept out more of the soft powdery snow. Although, being a town where practicality had to come first, many of the women refused to lose sight of their feminine side completely and because of this, sales of lace, ribbon and bright coloured buttons increased quite dramatically once Caitlin had been put in charge of their procurement.

These things did not happen very rapidly because, depending on the weather and the time of year, it took anywhere from three to six months for an order to arrive from England, but David and Caitlin were prepared to wait because they could see there was good money to be made as long as they bought wisely. Supplies of Virginian tobacco were decidedly erratic due to the attempted blockade of all things American by the French, but when it was obtainable, it always sold well to the native inhabitants, settlers and sailors alike. Although an inferior type could be grown in the most sheltered valleys of Newfoundland almost everybody preferred the real thing.

As her life became filled with more and more fresh ideas and she found new friends, the shy, timid girl who had arrived in St John's almost entirely disappeared. Caitlin was now a happy, confident, laughing young woman who had made the town her home and her destiny. She was beginning to forget about the bad times of the past, though even now, sometimes in the dark hours of the night, the old terrors would come creeping back unwanted. She would see the dead faces of her Father, Uncle and Grandmother or remember the cold, numb misery of the times in the minister's house in Oban. Sometimes, if the awful visions and demons really gripped her mind she would go and creep into bed with Mary, or with the children, if the lieutenant was home from sea. She would not disturb them, just the reassurance of another friendly creature, albeit a sleepy one helped to make the nightmares diminish until sleep overcame her again. Despite these occasional flash backs, she never thought about or analysed her situation. She lived her life day by day, taking each new challenge as it came to her and dealing with it as best she could. She didn't think about the future, today was good and that was all she needed.

The money she had owed to Mary had long since been returned and there was even a little left over for herself after her board and lodging had been paid. She had her new family, a few good friends in the town and at the store, but she could never quite forget the promise she had made that day on the mountainside overlooking her home. There was nothing she could do, in fact she didn't know really what it was she wanted to achieve. Something had been taken away from her that day and she alone was responsible for keeping alive the need for atonement. Hatred, revenge or punishments were not in her heart, more a restoration of things past and a recognition of wrongs committed. She was growing up and she was happier than she had been at any time since she had been forced from her home in the glen.

CHAPTER TEN

She was totally unprepared when, about two and a half years after Caitlin had arrived in St John's, David Harrison, the owner of the store, called her into his office just after the store had closed for the night. All the other staff had left, but Caitlin, conscientious as usual had stopped behind for a few minutes to make up some orders that would have to be delivered just as soon as the shop opened the next morning.

"Ah yes, Caitlin. Come in. Please sit down."

David Harrison rose from his desk came round to the side where Caitlin was sitting, perched himself somewhat awkwardly on the front corner and looked down at the girl.

A tall slim man he had an air of frailty about him that belied his strength and stamina. At thirty six years of age, his hair was thinning and turning grey, but he still had a twinkle in his eye, a ready smile and a kind word for everybody. He was possessed of a vitality and energy that drove him on to succeed and although this meant he was constantly busy doing something in or around the store, he would always have time to talk to the people who worked for him, being courteous and respectful to all the women, native or pioneer alike. Through his enormous hard work, considerable skill and, drawing on the experience gained during the years working in his family's business and making good use of the advice and encouragement that arrived from his father in Bristol with every consignment of goods, he had made a success of the enterprise. As he ruefully put it, he had become a glorified grocer after all.

"I expect you are wondering what this is all about. Don't look so worried my dear, you aren't in any trouble, and you've done nothing wrong. I asked you to come in here because I have something I want to ask you."

He paused for a moment.

"We've spent a lot of time working together since you came here over two years ago and I've seen you grow up and change from a rather awkward and very timid girl into a beautiful young woman. You are extremely clever and have become a great asset to the store. And," he added, "to me."

After a moment's hesitation, he continued.

"The business has been doing extremely well recently and that's due in no small part to you and your efforts. The customers would much rather have you serve them than any of the other assistants and, well…."

He stopped again as if he was trying to find the right words.

"I've come to enjoy your company very much. I've never looked forward to coming to the store each morning as much as I have since you came to work here. I'm thirty six now and would dearly love to have someone to pass the store on to when I get older. So I wonder if you would consider becoming my wife? I know you're young but I think you are mature enough to make a good decision."

Caitlin didn't say a word, but looked down at the floor, hoping that her hair, as it fell forwards beside her face, would hide her blushes; for although she would never admit it, even to herself, she had become very fond of her employer and had looked at him more than once with misty eyes when she knew he wasn't looking.

The young and the not so young men of St John's certainly had not failed to notice the beautiful and capable young girl in their town. Although she chatted to them all and had even mildly flirted with one or two, she hadn't had any great desire for any of these encounters to go any further or become serious. She felt that she wasn't really ready for any further changes in her life and also, her feelings towards David had been getting stronger day by day, though even in her wildest dreams she never thought that she would ever hear him say the words that he had just spoken.

"You don't have to give me an answer straight away, but I hope you will give the matter some thought and let me know soon. I do hope so very much that you will agree to my proposal."

As soon as David uttered the word 'proposal', Caitlin panicked. For some strange reason the word had more impact on her than the request that she should become his wife. With a gasp she leapt to her feet and ran from the room. Without stopping to gather up her purse or put on her bonnet, she hurried straight out of the store, along the streets and back to the garrison on the hill above the town. People stared at her as she rushed past, but she was totally oblivious to their presence. She didn't stop until she reached the little cot behind the curtain in the bedroom in Mary's house. Her mind was in turmoil. The comfortable and stable life into which she had at last settled had been shattered and completely turned upside down.

As she lay curled up in a little ball, buried beneath the blankets, her confused mind kept remembering all the frightening times she had been through in the last three years or so; the horror of finding the burnt bodies of her family, the misery of her time in the cave above her family home in the glen, the freezing cold and bone-aching weariness of the nights in the loft at the minister's house in Oban. All these dramatic events came back to her and in her confused state and although, obviously, David's proposal of marriage was not dangerous in any way, the prospect of another enormous change, was more than her brain and her adolescent emotions could cope with.

When Caitlin did not appear for the evening meal, Mary went to look for her, and upon finding her buried under the covers in her bed was very concerned that she was not feeling well, but when she saw the crumpled, tearstained face of her little friend appearing from under the bedclothes she realised that any problems that Caitlin might have were emotional rather than physical.

"My dear, whatever is the matter?" Asked Mary with concern.

Caitlin did not reply, but kneeled up on the bed, flung her arms around Mary's neck and burst into tears again. The older woman held her tight and whilst waiting patiently for the weeping to subside, thought of the young, innocent, frightened girl she had held on board the sailing ship off the Scottish Coast, little more than two and a half years ago. Since then, both their lives had changed out of all recognition.

Together they had faced many daunting prospects and overcome new challenges. Although Mary seemed to be the self-assured one, many times Caitlin's mere presence and her air of practicality had given the older woman the strength and confidence to continue. She had had Henry, of course, but he had a very down-to-earth attitude that wasn't a great deal of help when she herself felt stressed or depressed. Now, by complete coincidence and for very different reasons, both their lives were going to be changed again; but this time, though Caitlin didn't know it yet, circumstances were dictating that they would have to go their separate ways.

"It's Mr Harrison. He's asked me to marry him but I don't want to leave you and the children but I don't want to upset him either because I think he's really nice and I don't know what to do and I'm scared."

The words tumbled out, and as if the uttering of them seemed to make them even more frightening than before, the tears flowed again.

As the crying died down to a few subdued snuffles, Mary reached into her sleeve and pulled out a large handkerchief which she handed to Caitlin and said lightly.

"Is that all? I thought it was something serious. Nothing to be scared of, you silly goose. I have seen that that was coming for quite some time. It appears to me that you have made quite an impression on your boss. There are plenty of other girls in this town who would be only too glad to become his wife; I should take him up on his offer quickly, before he changes his mind."

Mary hesitated a moment before continuing.

"You've been thinking about him a lot lately haven't you?"

"Yes" said Caitlin softly. "I think he's lovely but I don't know if I'm good enough for him. I'm not smart and sophisticated like some of the other women that I know he's friendly with. Like Sarah Briggs. Her father has a whole fleet of fishing boats and she dresses like she's going to a party every day. You know I haven't got any money for a dowry. I'm only a poor country girl from Scotland. So why does he want to marry me?"

"Don't belittle yourself Caitlin. If I know David Harrison, he won't want a wife just to keep her in pretty clothes and put her on a pedestal. By the way the store looks these days; I don't think he needs your money either. No, I'm certain he is after somebody with a brain and a bit of character. He will want a partner not a puppy."

Mary paused and thought to herself . 'Now is as good a time as any to make my own surprising announcement. Might as well get all the agitation over at the same time.'

She took a deep breath.

"And anyway there is something else I have to talk to you about. I've got some news of my own." Mary continued. "I didn't want to tell you before, because everything was only finally confirmed this morning, after you had gone to the store." She paused again to make sure that Caitlin was paying attention to what she was saying and had not gone back to fretting about her own great news.

"Henry has just been told that he has been promoted to captain and that the Navy is sending him to the West Indies to take command of a fort in Jamaica. It is a great step up for him and he will be paid much more than he was as a lieutenant, but he doesn't think it's safe for me and the children to go with him. There's still a lot of trouble down there with the French and he says that there are plenty of buccaneers and pirates in the area attacking any ship they find. So he's arranged for all of us to go back to England to live with his family near a place called Rochester in the south of England. Henry and I had both sort of assumed that you would be coming with us, but after what you have just told me I don't think that'll happen now."

Mary sighed.

"It seems to me that your future and your destiny are here in St John's and not back in England with me and the children."

At this new revelation, another pillar of security was destroyed for Caitlin. Everything she knew and had striven to build was being torn apart. She couldn't see that a new life was beginning for her; marriage, a husband and exciting times were just around the corner. All she could see was a huge darkness looming before her. Her face dropped and her eyes filled with tears, but before she could dissolve into weeping again, Mary said firmly,

"We'll have no more of that nonsense. A girl who has just had a proposal of marriage shouldn't be crying. You couldn't have lived with us for ever and become an old maid. Now blow your nose and tell me everything."

"But what are you going to do without me?" Caitlin asked. "I'm part of the family now."

"Don't you worry about me my dear. Once I get back to England I shall have Henry's family to help me. Henry tried to get everything arranged before he told me so that I didn't have to worry about things back in England. In a letter that he received from them just this morning they told him that they will be very pleased to see me and will give me all the help I need. They say they have even found a little cottage that they think will suit me and the children just fine".

"But what about marrying David? Will I be a good wife? Can I do all the things he will expect of me? How will I manage without you? What about Angelina and Malcolm?" The questions came tumbling out as Caitlin struggled to envisage what future lay ahead.

The two women talked far into the night, interrupted only by the need to put the children to bed and Caitlin's need for food. Matters were discussed at enormous length and her fears of the unknown subsided as Caitlin realised that this was an amazing opportunity for her to better herself and to be with the man with whom she was falling in love. By the time she went to bed, with help, support and advice from Mary, negative thoughts had given way to excitement and anticipation. By the time the dawn began to turn the eastern sky to red, Caitlin had decided what she was going to do.

When she left for work the next morning, Caitlin was wearing her best dress, indeed her only one that was not designed for everyday working use. It was made of the softest wool and was the brightest cherry red, with wide sleeves and a white lace collar. Until now she had only worn it a few times and then only on special occasions. Although she felt a little self-conscious when she wore the dress, it was her pride and joy. She had bought it at the biggest clothes shop in St John's three months previously with money she had saved from her wages.

Before leaving the garrison, Mary had helped her to brush her hair, and though still leaving it loose, had tied it to one side with a ribbon the colour of burnished gold. The effect was amazing. She was transformed from the young shop girl into a woman of great beauty; enhanced of course, by the radiance and excitement of a girl about to give her answer to a proposal of marriage. She carried with her a large bag that contained her everyday working clothes.

Unlike the red dress, they were plain and utilitarian; much more suitable for her work in the store.

Although she was slightly earlier than usual arriving for work, David Harrison, always the first to arrive at the store, eager as he was for an answer to this question, had still arrived before her. When he saw Caitlin enter the room his face broke into a large smile and he hurried across to meet her holding out both hands in greeting.

"Good morning Caitlin. You look very fine this morning. I do hope your choice of dress indicates that you have some good news for me. And your hair!" He left the sentence unfinished.

Caitlin smiled back and taking both his hands in hers, looked straight into his eyes in such a way that his heart skipped a beat, and said softly,

"Good Morning to you too Mr Harrison. You too look very smart. I've been thinking all night about your offer and as you will probably have guessed I have talked to Mary about what you said to me. But before I give you my answer I want you to understand a few things that you may not have heard about, but that have happened to me in the past and which have influenced the person I have become."

David knew that Caitlin was Scottish and that she and her family had been dispossessed. He knew too that Mary had been her saviour, taking the girl under her wing and bringing her to Canada without knowing much about her. But he had no idea of most of the terrible things that had happened to her family, or about the horrible time she had spent in Oban. So he let her speak without interruption.

She spoke calmly and clearly about what had actually happened that day in the glen. She told him of the horror of seeing her house burn and of watching as her uncle was brutally murdered just for a yellow metal candlestick. She tried to describe the sense of feeling so utterly alone in the world with nowhere to turn for help because she had known nobody from outside the village. David was amazed at her resourcefulness and fortitude under such huge stress, and when she finished by telling him of her resolve to somehow right the wrongs that had taken place that day, his respect for her integrity was boundless.

As soon as David realized she had come to the end of her story, he gently let go of her hands, turned and walked slowly back to his desk and quietly sat down. He thought for a minute and looking at Caitlin he said,

"Thank you for telling me all this. I can see that it must be difficult to talk about it and bring things that you would rather leave hidden back to the surface. But you are absolutely right to tell me. It's no good starting off relationships with secrets. I think one of the reasons you decided to reveal these horrible things was to give me a chance to change my mind before it's too late; however your story has had just the opposite effect on me. Your honesty and openness has convinced me even further that you are the person with whom I want to spend the rest of my life. So, please put me out of my misery and give me your answer."

"My answer to you, David, is yes. But you have to understand that there are certain things I must insist upon that may seem to you rather unconventional. I want to be fully involved in your business and the direction it takes, I want our children, if there are to be any, to be given a broad education, and in particular any girls we may have. I will do my best to be a good wife to you and I wish that our marriage will be a union of minds as well. I know that I am still only very young but in the short life that I have had already, I have travelled a great distance through life as well as the world and I couldn't bear to just become the little woman at home waiting for her husband to return."

As she spoke, Caitlin ticked off each statement on her fingers because she was determined not to forget any of the things that she had thought of during the past wakeful night. When she was finished, she let her hands fall to her sides as she instinctively waited for David to make the next move. She had been somewhat reticent about using David's first name when she gave him her answer but decided that if they were going to be man and wife, she might as well start using it straight away.

David stood up, crossed the room and stood in front of Caitlin but without touching her, he said,

"My dearest, I too have made great journeys in my life, though none as dreadful as those that you have been through. I pray to God that our individual paths may now be joined together and become one wider, smoother highway. I know that all roads have hills and descents and many other obstacles, but those crossed with joy, compassion and true love, as well as hard work and understanding, can be travelled more easily when travelled together."

One look and one small step forward by them both was all that was needed to dispel any doubts in their minds.

CHAPTER ELEVEN

A few breathless minutes later, Caitlin broke away, brushed the hair from her face and said briskly,

"I must go and change into my other clothes. The store won't open itself."

Caitlin disappeared into the chandlery to put on her workday clothes and to busy herself with the practicalities of opening up the store for the day. Others could have done this but she had taken it upon herself to unlock the doors and remove the shutters from the windows every morning about a year after she had started working there. Nobody could have failed to notice the big smile on her face that day and the glow of happiness that she could not hide had she even wanted to. David stood for a moment looking at the door that had just closed behind the greatest change that his life would ever experience, then turned and went back to his desk where he sat down deep in thought but eminently content.

The stipulation that she would take an active role in the business did not really come as a great surprise to David. She was already doing a lot of the day to day management, though always deferring to him to make the final decisions. His only concern was how it would affect his standing in a small, colonial and somewhat conservative society that expected a man to be in complete control of his business affairs. Women were expected to be subservient to

their husbands, particularly in regard to financial matters. After
some thought, he decided to discuss the problem quite openly
with Caitlin and to suggest to her that he was happy to agree to
her suggestions, but that they should let it appear to those on the
outside that he was the one who made the important decisions
and was the driving force behind things, as convention expected.
Having decided on this course of action, David left the office to join
Caitlin in the store where she was already busy with the customers.

During a quiet period later in the day, when there was an opportunity for them to be alone together, he broached the subject of
her involvement, and so after considerable discussion, which took
much longer than it should due to numerous, wonderful, heady
interruptions for kisses, it was agreed that she would at least for the
time being allow the community to see that she was answerable
to him, whilst he would teach her all he could about accountancy
and share with her the financial details of his business. Little did
they know that the financial knowledge she would learn would be
put to good use much sooner than they could have ever guessed.

When Caitlin returned home that night, Mary did not need
to be told of the outcome of the day. Caitlin's radiant smile said it
all; dispelling any doubts and misgivings that Mary had had about
leaving behind the girl that she had come to regard as her daughter,
alone in a foreign land when she herself returned to live in England.
Flinging her arms round the younger girl, she demanded to be told
immediately all the details of the day, and called to her husband
and the children to come and share in the good news.

The next few days were a mixture of emotional highs and lows
for everybody; great excitement about the forthcoming wedding but
also deep sadness over Mary's departure. For a time, it was Caitlin's
turn to give encouragement to the older friend. Mary seemed very
depressed about returning to England just when she had got herself
settled in St John's but when Caitlin pointed out that it would be

another adventure and probably give the children more opportunities in life, Mary cheered up and began to be much more positive about the forthcoming relocation. Even though they had only been friends for a little while and their ages were separated by over a decade, Mary and Caitlin had become totally devoted to each other and had come to rely on each other for so much.

With no reason to delay the marriage, there followed a few hectic weeks of preparation for an autumn celebration. It suited everybody concerned to hold the wedding fairly quickly, in part due to their wish to be married before the storms of winter prohibited the guests that they wanted to invite but who lived at any distance, from attending; but also because of the imminent departure of Mary and the children. Henry was due to sail to the West Indies some time before Christmas and wanted to see his family off on their way home before he left. Caitlin had insisted on Mary being able to be there at the celebration, because, as she put it. "I won't feel married if my second mother isn't there to see me married."

Wearing the best suit of the finest cloth that his store could provide and made by the most accomplished tailor in St John's, David Harrison was an impressive, elegant figure as he waited at the altar of the little church on the hillside above the town; but he was entirely eclipsed by his bride-to-be as she walked down the aisle on the arm of the newly-promoted Captain Blake, who was resplendent in full ceremonial uniform. She was wearing a full length, soft, creamy-white woollen dress made for her by some of the local Indian women and a white lace mantilla lent to her by an Italian friend. The simplicity and muted colours of her outfit accentuated her youthful grace and beauty.

The wedding ceremony was a joyous occasion, simple and moving with guests from every background, race, colour and creed. From land and sea, the new world and the old one, they had all gathered to offer David and Caitlin their best wishes and to see them started on the pathway of married life. As a man of some substance David was well respected throughout the town and probably some of the more affluent ladies had expected that he would take as a bride a girl from one of the their own families. Because of her lowly status as a shop assistant, a number of people, especially women, had simply come to the church to get a glimpse of the woman David was marrying. Not that anybody disliked Caitlin herself, indeed, the ladies of the town who shopped in Harrison's store would remark just how pleasant and efficient an assistant she had become. Her marriage to David however meant that there was one less eligible bachelor in the town from whom their daughters could chose a husband.

At the nuptial feast the fare was simple and delicious. The festivities and dancing went on far into the night. Old friendships were rekindled and new ones begun. Men and women, adults and children all joined in with the celebrations and merrymaking .Such grand gatherings were an uncommon occurrence in the region and all those present certainly made the most of the occasion.

After three wonderful days and nights, alone in a tiny, remote fisherman's hut which they had been loaned, David and Caitlin returned to the store full of enthusiasm and new ideas. But before she could settle down to her new role as wife of the proprietor, she had to help Mary with the packing of all her belongings for her trip back to England.

It was a sad day when Caitlin stood on the dockside and with a heavy heart watched as the ship that was carrying her best friend away, disappear round the headland. David stood beside her with his arm around her waist and when there was nothing left to see across the water, she turned to him and looking up at him, her eyes wet with tears, her voice husky with emotion whispered,

"You are my only life now."

With Mary gone, Caitlin did not allow herself to feel lonely. She wrote long letters to her friend and was delighted to receive equally long replies, but she was by now quite capable of living her own life and although she realised how much Mary had done for her, she no longer needed the assurances and moral support that she had so desperately needed before.

As well as enjoying the delights of matrimony, she busied herself with making a complete inventory of the entire contents of the store. This was an enormous task because of the vast range and quantity of goods they had to stock to supply a growing nation. Most of the shipments from England arrived in late summer to avoid the worst of the Atlantic weather in winter and to ensure that they had sufficient supplies to last them all until the winter snows had melted and the worst of the storms had subsided.

Caitlin was a born trader; she was never happier than when she was out in the store, chatting cheerfully to the customers, actual or potential, trying to get a good deal on her purchases and a profit on her sales. But she believed in being fair and honest with everyone whether buying or selling, often quoting the old adage, "A satisfied customer may bring you another, but an unhappy one will take away ten you already have." Her ability to communicate with people in their own language helped enormously, with many people, particularly native Indians being prepared to wait for some time just to be served by someone who could understand what they wanted without actually having to point to an item. All this helped sales to rise far above levels that David had been able to achieve when working on his own.

Most of the trading with the local Indian people of the island of Newfoundland was for furs. Fox, wolf and mink were the most common ones presented for exchange, with a smaller percentage of beaver than would be found further west on the mainland. Seals however, made up the shortfall with the white new-born seal pup furs being particularly sought after.

The fur trade was well provided for by buyers from some of the biggest companies in North America with the Hudson's Bay

Company handling more furs than the rest of the traders put together. These companies considered that they had a monopoly in trading for furs and any new entrants to their market were vigorously discouraged. 'Sharp practises,' 'accidental fires' and 'unfortunate accidents' seemed to happen when a new and enthusiastic entrepreneur tried to enter the fur trade. David had been farsighted enough, as soon as he had begun trading to work out an agreement with the Hudson's Bay Company to act as a middleman between some of the trappers and themselves; he would not try to export the furs himself but would pass them on to the company only taking a small profit whilst they would not interfere with his ships' chandlery business. This may seem a somewhat dubious way to trade, but it was deemed acceptable at the time.

There was however another and as yet untapped local commodity that was suddenly in great demand. Sugar. Huge quantities were already being produced in the tropical climate of the West Indies where the hot and often damp climate of the Caribbean was ideally suited to the production of sugar cane grown mainly on large plantations that relied almost entirely upon slave labour. Huge fortunes were being made for the European plantation owners by the grinding hard labour of the black slaves that had been torn from their home environment, mainly on the west coast of Africa. However great financial risks, had to be taken to transport the sugar across the Atlantic and back to the shores of Europe. If a large shipment of sugar from one plantation was lost, by the perils of the sea or to piracy, a whole year's production and profit was destroyed in one accident. There had always been the threat of hurricanes throughout the Caribbean, particularly between July and October, but now, with political unrest and wars with France, a voyage at any time of the year was dangerous. Although the French warships were to be avoided whenever possible, it was the privateers and other pirates who were the greatest threat of all. They roamed the

Caribbean in their small, heavily armed frigates, ready to fight and plunder any vessel they could intercept regardless of its country of origin. The lawless captains of these destructive vessels paid lip service to the principles of whichever country suited them, but were only interested in making a fortune for themselves, paying no heed to the misery and suffering of those from whom they stole. Huge profits were to be made by the 'diversion' of cargoes of sugar to 'an alternative destination'.

The sugar produced in the north east of the American continent is in the form of maple syrup; which is the sap of the maple tree from which most of the water has been removed. The harvest period for the syrup is the middle to the end of winter when the sap is beginning to rise in the aptly named sugar maple trees that cloak the hills of Eastern Canada, Newfoundland, and the north eastern corner of the United States. To gather the sap, a small hole is drilled in the trunk of the maple tree and a short pipe is inserted to allow the liquid to run out into a container ready for collection. Once sufficient of the clear thin sap has been collected, it is placed in a wide-topped metal pan that has been placed over a fire and gently heated to allow most of the water to be evaporated. The residual viscous golden coloured liquid is maple syrup; a pure and natural form of sweetness that has been tapped from the trees by local Indian nations for centuries. Maple syrup can be eaten in its natural state or included in cooking.

With their local knowledge and experience gained over countless generations, the native people knew just where the best places were to collect the sap easily and quickly. Especially during the cold months of winter when nourishment was sometimes in short supply, this delicious, very sweet and sticky source of energy was an important part of their diet.

With her skills as a linguist, Caitlin was able to converse with people from many of the indigenous tribes who had made their homes in Newfoundland. Of particular interest to her were the conversations with the women, who, although outwardly subservient to their menfolk, actually had considerable influence on most domestic matters and were highly knowledgeable about the collection of wild vegetables, seeds and berries that were an important supplement to the meat and fish brought into the settlements from the forests and rivers by the hunters. It was these conversations that gave Caitlin the idea of persuading the local people to harvest the maple syrup and sell it to her, just as the Hudson's Bay Company were doing with the furs.

Once the germ of the idea had come to Caitlin, she asked as many questions of the local people as she could and discovered that the forests could provide quite a surplus of the sweet substance beyond the requirements as a food source for the local inhabitants. The main problem was that it was not easy to evaporate all the excess water away without burning the residue. The process had to be carried out slowly. Caitlin reasoned that if she could provide large flat bottomed iron pans, the maple syrup could be made more easily and in much larger quantities. Wood to fuel the process was readily available from the surrounding forests. If she could persuade local women to purchase these pans from her and let them pay for them out of the first batches of syrup they brought to her, she would have a scarce commodity to send back to England quite cheaply. Ship owners were only too glad to get anything they could to fill the holds of their ships on the return voyage to Europe, so her own freight charges should be quite small.

When Caitlin suggested the idea of trading in maple syrup to her husband, as they sat beside the fire one evening, his first reactions were not very encouraging.

"Don't you think we have enough to occupy us at the moment? Isn't it enough to have just got married and for you to be learning about the management of the store? Don't forget we still have to find ourselves a proper house. I'm not against the idea, but perhaps now isn't the right time." He suggested cautiously.

"Oh don't be silly." Caitlin replied impatiently. "It will take at least six months before the evaporating pans arrive from England and at least another six before we get any syrup coming in to the store. Besides," she added. "we've still got to convince the natives to trade it with us."

"That will have to be your task my dear. You know how much better you are at talking to them than I; especially with the women. They seem to stop talking whenever I'm around."

"That's just because you're a man and you don't try to talk to them in their own language. I think they're a bit afraid of you. I know you don't mean to be, but I'm sure they feel slightly intimidated"

"Hmmph."

There was a long pause .Caitlin bent over the coat she was mending for David whilst her husband stared silently into the flames. Finally he broke the silence.

"Very well my dear, Let us proceed with your unusual scheme. I'm not fully convinced that it will succeed but you seem to be able to make all your other ideas prosper. I think that the sugar business should be run separately from the store. If nothing else, it will give you some experience in running a business by yourself. I will give you any help you need but its success will be entirely up to you."

Caitlin put down her sewing, crossed the room and slid her hands lovingly round her husband's neck.

"Thank you for letting me try this out my love. I'm sure that it will work. I will start on the order for pans in the morning. But tonight…" She had no need to finish the sentence.

CHAPTER TWELVE

C aitlin ordered, with David's approval, ten of the large shallow evaporating pans for the processing of maple tree sap. These had to be ordered then shipped from England but she managed to despatch her request on the last ship crossing the ocean that autumn. Delivery next spring would allow her to get the evaporating pans deployed into the maple forests during the summer and autumn for use during the next winter with the first shipment of maple syrup to Europe ready to be shipped to England the following spring.

In his bachelor days, before his marriage to Caitlin, David had been content to live in a couple of converted store rooms upstairs in the warehouse, in effect; "above the shop". After the wedding, Caitlin had moved out of the garrison and into David's little apartment, but despite her natural ability to make almost anywhere into a home, the rooms just weren't big enough for the two of them so they had to find somewhere else to live quite quickly. David was all in favour of having a new house built on the slopes of Signal Hill above the entrance to St John's harbour in an area that was becoming popular with the more 'respectable' sector of society. But Caitlin would have none of it. She insisted that it was part of her grand plan for the expansion of the business that they purchase a much more modest house only a few yards from the store.

"We are going to spend a lot of time working in the store over the next few years and it makes sense for us to be close at hand rather than having to travel out of the town and back every day."

Wisely reasoning that Caitlin was not to be moved on this matter, David acquiesced and shortly after their marriage they managed to buy, at a reasonable price, a small but well-constructed house on the next street up the hill that ran parallel to the road on which the store was situated. It was not very large but suited their purposes. The small yard and back garden of their new house were immediately behind their own commercial premises, so it was a simple matter to create a walkway through from their own backyard into the rear of the store. It did not take them long to move all their modest belongings from above the store whilst Caitlin, yet again, started the task of turning a house into a home. How she wished Mary could have been with her to help her choose curtains, furniture and all the other domestic trappings and to share in her good fortune.

In addition to enjoying the exhilarating experiences and inevitable disagreements of newly married life, Caitlin and David worked tirelessly through the long winter, not only continuing with the already established business of the store but also in the planning and preparation of the new enterprises that Caitlin had in mind. David did his best to lead his wife through some of the intricacies and requirements of accountancy. Although she found figures extremely baffling, and never fully understood the rows and rows of numbers that lined the page, she was able to grasp sufficient knowledge to ensure that every change she made to the business of the store would produce some margin of profit.

Little more could be done that year to further the production of maple syrup, except to try and persuade the local people to bring the sweet and sticky substance to them and to ensure they understood why she needed, what was to them, such huge quantities. The syrup would be shipped in barrels containing about forty gallons, so it would take an enormous amount of the weak sap to produce enough of the delicious sweetness for her to make a worthwhile shipment. The much larger volumes that Caitlin needed to make a success of her export business could not be produced without many more of the evaporating pans that would not be available to them until the following season. Even any correspondence with potential buyers of the syrup in England was a very protracted affair due to the length of time letters took to reach their destination and for replies to be received. Communication across the Atlantic by sailing ship simply took a long time.

However the newlyweds thoroughly enjoyed the testing and tasting of the small quantities that they could obtain from the local people. Caitlin had never had a house of her own before and took great pleasure cooking and baking puddings and cakes with the syrup. David in turn took great pleasure in praising her efforts and thoroughly enjoyed consuming the tasty offerings.

One morning early in March, Caitlin asked her husband to open the store for her as she was not feeling very well. This was quite unlike her, because she was usually in the best of health and would never allow any minor ailments to keep her from the store. He was concerned for her but she said she would try to come down and help in the shop as soon as she felt better. When she finally appeared in David's office just before lunchtime, David saw that she was looking better but slightly pale and drawn. Caitlin walked round and stood beside her husband and resting her hand on his shoulder said quietly.

"I think you had better prepare yourself for a bit of a shock David. A good one but a shock nonetheless. Today wasn't the first time I've felt sick in the morning. And I think it won't be the last."

"Whatever do you mean?"

His wife giggled.

"Can't you guess dearest? Sometime in late summer or early autumn we are going to become parents. I hope it will be the little boy that you want so much."

For a moment, David stared at his wife, his mouth wide open, then, suddenly, with an astounded look on his face, he stood up so quickly that the chair in which he had been sitting fell over backwards with a crash. He turned, faced Caitlin and grasped her by the shoulders.

"Promise me you're not joking?"

Caitlin laughed and put her arms around the astonished man.

"Don't be silly. Do I have to spell it out to you?" She paused. "David Harrison. You are going to become a father in about seven months' time. I'm pregnant."

Now that he understood exactly what his wife was telling him, her usually, moderate and sober husband, gave a whoop of joy, grasped his wife around the waist and swung her round and around in delight. When he finally stopped, she gasped and asked if he wanted to make her sick again; but there was a twinkle in her eye. She was as pleased as he was.

They could not have kept the good news to themselves even if they had wished to. The beam on David's face, especially when he looked at his wife, made any announcement unnecessary, except as confirmation. He tried to make Caitlin take things a bit easier and to rest whenever she could; but she would have none of it.

"I am only having a baby. It's not the first time it's happened." She retorted, but as the summer heat progressed she found that she had to let her husband or other store assistants take over some of the roles that she had created for herself. She still sat in the store chatting to the customers, her hand resting lightly on her ever growing bulge. Everybody who came to the store, men and women, young and old, local inhabitant and settler, would greet her with a smile or come across for a friendly chat. All had come to love her and would chatter to her in whatever language was their native tongue. When the native women realised she was expecting, they would often bring little gifts for the baby when they came into the store, perhaps a wild gourd filled with seeds as a rattle, or a small wooden carving as a charm to bring the unborn child good luck.

How she missed Mary, a friend to chatter to, another woman to reassure her and with whom she could share the little moments of her growing child, such as when she first felt a tiny kick within her or when her usual pragmatic, down-to-earth nature was occasionally replaced by uncertainty. She did her best to share her excitement and fears with her old friend by sending her letters, written whenever she had a moment to herself, moments that became longer and longer as her ever-growing stomach prevented her from moving freely around the overfilled store.

Due to the usual transatlantic delay, Mary's letter, or rather several of her letters that arrived at once, could not have been more welcome because they were delivered just a few days before Caitlin's baby was born. As well as the usual congratulations and advice, Mary told her friend that she and the children were comfortably settled back in England and that Henry was expected home in about a year's time

Caitlin remained fit and well throughout her pregnancy, although the heat of midsummer was a trial to her in the last few months and finally in September, David, 'took delivery' as he put it, of a beautiful daughter. That day, there was no happier or delighted man in St John's than David Harrison.

They named her Margaret Mary. Margaret after Caitlin's mother and Mary after Mary Blake. "I will choose the names for the girls and you can choose for the boys," said Caitlin with a smile when the matter was discussed.

Margaret Mary was only about ten days old when her mother started to take her to the store with her. When David remonstrated with her that the baby was far too young, Caitlin retorted,

"Well, I don't see why. She can sleep just as well in her little crib next to me behind the counter as she can at home, and if she needs my attention, or I have to feed her, I will simply go upstairs to the room that you used to live in before we were married. It's not as if I will be the only person in the place. There are other assistants to take over when I have to look after her needs. And anyway." She concluded. "it's high time I came back, even for part of the time. The customers will to want to talk to me and to see the new baby."

She got her own way, of course and soon Margaret Mary was the greatest attraction the store had ever had; particularly for the native women because most of the white pioneer's children rarely appeared in public until they were old enough to walk. Mothers the world over are inquisitive about children from other shores. Even David, despite his original disapproval could often be seen bending over the crib and gazing down at his little daughter. There were times when Caitlin would have to remind him that there were other things that needed his attention and send him back to his tasks. He seemed to be concentrating less on his business and allowing his wife to undertake an ever-increasingly important role.

The sugar evaporation pans that had been ordered from England the previous autumn arrived in the late spring of that year and during the last weeks before the birth of her daughter; Caitlin had made arrangements for them to be to be taken up into the hills in preparation for the next winter's maple syrup collection season. Barrels that were small enough to be slung from a stout pole and carried by two people were prepared to accompany the pans. These would be filled and returned whereas the pans would remain with the local women, considering that they were, or would be when paid for, their own property.

Before selecting the sites to which to send the pans, Caitlin talked to some of the native women who would be likely to do much of the work that went into harvesting the maple syrup. By listening to all their tales of syrup collection she was able to select what she thought were the best parts of the island for her purposes. Obviously there had to be plenty of sugar maple trees but also the resulting syrup had to be transported back to St John's and this could only realistically be done by water; down the rivers or by sea, or a combination of both. It would be impracticable to try to haul the heavy, filled barrels overland where there were no proper roads across the high ridges that separated the beautiful wooded valleys where the sugar maples grew. The birch bark canoes used throughout the region were superlative craft for use in the rivers, very strong and perfectly adequate for the barrels and light enough for portage around the rapids, but they were not very suitable for use at sea. She also made sure that those people receiving the pans understood how they were to be used; if the syrup was boiled for too long, the sugar would be caramelised and burnt rendering the entire batch worthless. Caitlin also asked one of the local coopers, the barrel makers, to show some of the natives how to fill and seal the casks so that they were secure and the precious contents would be safe on the perilous journey down the rivers and along the coast to St John's. Maple syrup will not deteriorate for many years if it is sufficiently concentrated, so there was no need for any preservatives to be included.

It was decided that the ten pans would be despatched to five separate valleys so that there would be a reasonable capacity at each place to fill the barrels but also to make certain that not so much sap would be taken from the trees in one area that they would not be able to produce again in subsequent seasons.

Unfortunately the enterprise suffered a considerable loss when, two of the pans were destroyed when a canoe carrying them capsized whilst being towed up some rapids, but the remainder managed to reach their destination with little more than a few dents and scratches. Traditionally the natives would simply have unloaded their goods and carried them, and the canoes around any obstacle, but with the arrival of sailors from the European ships who had the knowledge and skills to make longer and stronger rope from locally grown plants, such as hemp, the practise of towing canoes up rapids was used more and more frequently. This was much less laborious and time-consuming, but also carried far greater risk of disaster. As a consequence of this, quite a number of the wonderfully constructed and precious canoes as well as their hard won cargoes were lost.

During the late winter and early spring, despite having her hands full with the needs of a new baby, an increasingly successful store and an ever more forgetful husband, the first consignment arrived from the woods. There was enough syrup for her to transfer the sugary liquid from the smaller containers into three larger barrels, each of about forty gallons, and to despatch them to the Mr Harrison senior in Bristol on the first vessel to depart from Newfoundland that spring. He was able to use his contacts in the grocery business to publicise Caitlin's new importation. Despite a certain degree of resistance to the idea that sugar could be produced from the sap of trees, all the maple syrup sold at a good price.

CHAPTER THIRTEEN

Due to the difficulties of supply and the ever increasing demand for sweetness at that time, prices for sugar were at an all-time high, and although the flavour of maple syrup differed somewhat from that of the cane sugar from the West Indies, the merchants demanded that she send them as much of the new product as she could obtain as soon as possible.

At her request, the profits due to her from the sale of her syrup were sent back across the ocean in the form of more evaporating pans and some filtration equipment to enable her to export a more refined syrup. Encouraged by this favourable beginning, and with the addition of many more evaporating pans delivered that summer Caitlin was able to increase the shipment the following year to forty barrels. Now that the initial hesitancy for her product had waned, the sugar merchants could not get enough of the syrup and demand always seemed to outstrip supply.

Despite the fact that Caitlin was proving beyond doubt that a woman was perfectly capable of running a considerable business and although they already had a beautiful daughter, David was still convinced that he needed a son to whom he could leave the business. So he was highly delighted when Charles was born just after Margaret Mary's third birthday. There was much rejoicing from the whole family, with the little girl being highly delighted to have a baby brother in her life, fussing over him all the time as though she were his mother herself. David was pleased to name his new-born son after his own father who had been of such assistance to him in the initial years of his enterprise in St John's.

As Caitlin's pregnancy had progressed, David seemed to be becoming more and more forgetful. On more than one occasion he was seen going into the storeroom at the back of the shop then returning empty handed; he had no idea what he had gone to fetch. He could no longer be trusted to shut up the shop for the night or extinguish all the lamps. This all gave Caitlin another worry that she could well have done without.

Now that he appeared to have resolved the problem of his succession with the birth of his son, David seemed to 'Let Go' and appeared to allow his mental faculties to dissipate rapidly. Despite all the encouragement and stimulations of his friends and family, his mental state deteriorated very quickly and although he went through the motions of attending the store each day, in actual fact he was of very little use. Caitlin and all the other staff had to watch him carefully to make sure that he didn't do anything or forget any-thing that might cause accidents or even fires. Just as he had done when his daughter was newly born, he would often go and gaze at Charles in his cradle behind the counter in the store with great love and devotion; the difference this time however was that as soon as he was called away, he would simply return and watch the child again. He never attempted to pick up the child, he appeared to be content just to observe. He was never violent or aggressive; it just seemed that his confidence and vivacity were slowly fading away, as was his memory.

Although they didn't realise it at the time he was suffering from the onset of the early stages of dementia.

Caitlin worked tirelessly, but the burden of running the store, looking after two young children and being the protector of an increasingly forgetful and difficult husband, became more than even she was able to manage. She had no alternative but to look elsewhere for some assistance with the day-to-day running and administration of the store.

There were quite a number of competent and presentable candidates in St John's that would have been more than capable of fulfilling the role but, much to the surprise and consternation of almost the entire population and in a move that was totally unprecedented in the history of St John's, Caitlin engaged a native man as her assistant manager.

He was a member of the Adirondack tribe from slightly further south on the mainland who had been brought to the town several years earlier having suffered horrific injuries. Whereas most of the tribe had been aggressive towards the settlers, or at best indifferent, he had actually sought out the company of some soldiers who had been put ashore at the mouth of a large creek several hundred miles up the St Lawrence River. Their task had been to improve and secure a site that would be suitable for unloading military supplies. He had been persuaded to stay and help them unload some cargo when a ship arrived; probably with the incentive of a few gifts and alcohol. A crude wharf had been built and whilst a large gun was being unloaded it had slipped from its slings as it was being swung ashore, crashing down upon his legs as he waited to guide it on to a horse drawn waggon. With no proper medical attention available at the remote site where the accident happened, he was taken by the ship, when the unloading of her cargo was completed, to St John's, her next port of call. A naval surgeon from a British warship that happened to be in port at that time, sewed up his wounds and set the bones in crude splints and although his wounds were slow to heal and for a time, amputation seemed inevitable, he survived with both his legs intact.

With the recovery of his patient far from complete, and with his ship under orders to set sail for England, the surgeon left his patient in the caring hands of the women of St John's. Along with several other wives, Caitlin attended to his needs and dressed his wounds. She made sure that he was provided with all the available medication and food that the store could provide. It seemed natural to her to use her special ability to communicate with him as best she could in his native language. This was totally in keeping with her character, just as it had been Mary Blake's; to help those less fortunate than herself regardless of the cost. and to try to make sure that the peoples to whom the area had originally belonged were to some degree included in the creation of the new society that was emerging.

As he recovered, the young man expressed his gratitude by doing small jobs around the store and as his strength and physical abilities improved, generally making himself indispensable in an unassuming way. After a few months, a pronounced limp was the only sign that he had been injured, though it did mean that he would never be able to return to his village, to run and hunt in the forests as he would have done before. He was a quiet man with an enormous thirst for knowledge which Caitlin and, as far as he was able, David encouraged and during quiet periods within the store they were able to teach him to read and write and the basics of mathematics. His name was virtually unpronounceable to the European tongue, so from the outset of his residence in St John's he was simply known as Little Joe. He never wanted to return to his native land and when he could be persuaded to talk about it, which wasn't often, he would simply say,

"It was the New People that saved me from death, so it is with the New People I shall stay."

Realising that to simply hand over the reins to Little Joe would be courting disaster; Caitlin took her time introducing the new manager to her customers. Most of them already knew him from his activity in and around the store but it came as a surprise to them to see him taking on the greater role. Certainly a few of the diehard settlers thought that it was disgraceful and demeaning to see the other assistants taking instructions from a native man and took their custom elsewhere. But this was more than counteracted by the increase in trade from the indigenous population who were delighted to see one of their own countrymen taking over such an important position within the settler's world. It was nearly two years before Caitlin was satisfied that Little Joe was capable of managing the store on his own and even then she would oversee the largest of the shipments that came in from England.

Over the next few years, events continued to move rapidly for Caitlin. The children were a great source of delight to her as she continued to watch them grow and apart from the usual and expected childish tantrums, they caused her no problems. The store went from strength to strength, and continued to grow in popularity as her ever-increasing purchases of maple syrup provided the local people with a valuable commodity other than fur with which to trade, and although some of the revenue was regrettably used to purchase alcohol at the taverns down by the waterside, much of it was spent in her store on more mundane but necessary items thus giving her a closed cycle of profits.

In order to accommodate the increase in the supply of maple syrup, a greater and greater number of barrels were required for each shipment although several round trips could often be achieved from each one before it became unusable. Some of the materials that were shipped back to Canada in these barrels on the return voyage to make efficient use of the cargo space in the ships' holds made them unsuitable for a further shipments of syrup. For example, any iron goods placed in the barrels would react with the tannin in the oak staves causing staining that would be released when in contact with the sugary liquid. To overcome this shortfall of suitable barrels and also because she could see that the whaling industry with its insatiable requirement for barrels to hold all the oil, was rapidly growing, Caitlin set up a cooperage in a nearby warehouse for their manufacture and refurbishment. Whaling ships from Britain, Norway and along the eastern coast of America would come and discharge their precious cargo, replace any damaged equipment, take on board a stock of replacement barrels, replenish their food supplies and try to recruit suitable crew to take the place of any that had jumped ship in St John's.

The forests around St John's were able to provide an excellent supply of American white oak for this purpose. The knowledge and cooperation of the local tribes was essential for the selection and transportation of this timber and Caitlin's linguistic skills again played a crucial part in the successful negotiations. Coopers that she had persuaded to come over from England were soon producing enough barrels for the maple syrup and they were able to sell as many as they could make to the visiting whalers. With space on these ships being extremely cramped, the huge casks that were used for whale oil were loaded into the holds in a kind of kit form and when they were required, the on-board craftsmen would simply assemble however many barrels were needed.

So, with the store, maple syrup trade and the barrel making enterprises all inter-connecting and becoming highly successful, Caitlin was now a wealthy woman with considerable standing in the town. This enabled her to obtain and pay for the services of a private tutor for Margaret Mary and Charles. She knew that she had been extremely lucky to have escaped from the poverty and in some cases even the starvation that had been the fate of so many of her fellow countrymen who had suffered expulsion from their homes. She was determined that no child of hers would have the disadvantage a lack of education would bring. Material things were of far lesser importance to her than knowledge and she was deter-mined that her wealth would be better used in this way rather than on fine clothes and fancy houses.

Callum Logan, the man that Caitlin engaged to teach her children had been born in St John's. His father was the minister of the Scottish church in the town to which Caitlin had regularly taken Angelina and Malcolm when they all lived in the garrison before her marriage to David. Roderick Logan, the minister, wisely thinking that his son would get a better education in England, had sent Callum back to stay with relatives whilst he studied; first at a major grammar school followed by a scholarship to Edinburgh University where he read Law.

In assuming that his son would remain in England to pursue his own career, his father did not however take into account the young man's love of the land where he was born. Callum returned to St John's and re-joined his family. His father would have been happy for his son to enter the church and work alongside him but the young man decided that he was not suited to the life of a minister of religion. He searched for some kind of employment that would make good use of the excellent education his parents had provided for him and when he heard that Caitlin was seeking somebody to teach her children, he asked to be considered. Determined only to have the best teacher for her offspring, Caitlin made thorough checks into Callum's background and abilities before she was satisfied that he was what she was looking for.

She could not have made a better choice, because not only was he an extremely competent teacher but Margaret Mary and Charles soon came to love their tutor and he became very attached to his pupils. With his innate teaching skills and his ability to relate to children, they all enjoyed their lessons from the start.

Caitlin's wealth could also provide the care that David's deteriorating mental state required. His forgetfulness and obsession with trivialities had reached a point where he was actually of little use in the store or even in looking after the children. He would spend an hour deciding which pair of shoes to put on or whether he wanted an apple for dessert. To make his indecision worse, if somebody tried to make the decision for him or perhaps tell him to put on his coat before going outside, he would fly into the most terrible rage that was upsetting to others around him as well as to himself. He was never physically violent towards others and gradually descended into a little world of his own, mostly silent and unable to give or receive affection. This meant that there was little that could now be done for him other than to provide for his physical needs; food, clothing and hygiene and to try to protect him from coming to any harm. His unpredictability meant that he could never be left alone, day or night. Difficult though it must have been for David himself, it was probably even more distressing for those who loved and cared for him. Their feeling of helplessness was so great because there was nothing they could do to help or console him.

Towards the end he became totally preoccupied with searching for his little dog, Nemo. He had been a scruffy, battered mongrel who had attached himself to the storekeeper and who for years had been his constant companion whilst David had lived alone in the rooms above the store. Nemo had died of old age some years previously though David had never really accepted that he was gone. No amount of persuasion would convince him that the animal was dead. Finally on a bitterly cold winter's night, just as the store was closing, David eluded his protectors and disappeared into the darkness, presumably to look for his pet. Desperate attempts by Caitlin, her friends, the entire staff of the store and search parties organised by the townsfolk all failed to locate him. Soldiers from the garrison also became involved, but it was not until some days later that his frozen body was found on a thickly forested slope in the hills about five miles inland from the town.

Caitlin took the death of her husband remarkably calmly. In some ways it came as a relief; he had not been a husband to her or a father to their children for quite some time. She knew that his condition was nothing of her doing, but an insidious illness inside his brain from which there was no escape. It was only when she sat down on her own one evening to write a letter to David's relatives in Bristol to tell them of his death that her composure left her and the tears flowed. It was the usual self-assured woman who opened the store next morning. She would never let her misery show to the children or anybody outside the family.

Despite his deteriorating state of health over the last few years, David had still been a respected member of the community and as a result almost the entire town of St John's was present to bid him farewell at the simple but very moving funeral of one of their best known citizens.

Widowhood could have resulted in her withdrawal from the life that she had created for herself in the store, as might have been expected during these times when men reigned supreme. But this wasn't Caitlin. Possibly because over the previous few years, as David's mental condition had degenerated, she had got used to the idea of being on her own, emotionally if not physically. She still had the needs of her children to attend to and although Little Joe had become extremely proficient in his running of the little commercial empire that Caitlin had created, it was still necessary for her to oversee him, particularly when handling large sums of money and arranging transfers of funds when shipments of trading goods were imported. In the years since Caitlin had become involved in the store and in no small part due to her influence, Harrisons had grown to the point where it was now by far the largest ships' chandlers in St John's, creating, both directly and indirectly employment for several hundred people.

CHAPTER FOURTEEN

David's death occurred in the winter of 1815-16, shortly after the battle of Waterloo which effectively ended the Napoleonic wars. After this conclusive battle, the French soon brought an end to their blockade of the Caribbean's sugar trade. Although there could no longer be any pretence or excuse that they were sailing under letters of marque from either the French or the British, there were still plenty of pirates operating purely in their own interests who would attack and plunder any unprotected and un-armed merchant ship. However, the cessation of hostilities allowed for the deployment of more British naval ships to escort the merchantmen and to track down and destroy these predatory vessels.

In direct consequence of this, the price of sugar that could be imported from the Caribbean, which had almost trebled since the war with the French had begun, fell dramatically, causing the demand for Caitlin's maple syrup to disappear almost overnight. Cane sugar added very little flavour of its own to other foods and unlike maple syrup this ability, to increase the sweetness but not to alter the flavour of the food to which it was added increased its popularity quite significantly. The Caribbean could now produce and ship sugar at a far lower price, with the assistance of slave labour, than Caitlin could ever hope to achieve. The first shipment that Caitlin sent across to Bristol after trade with the West Indies resumed brought such a low price that she saw immediately there was nothing to be achieved by continuing to produce maple syrup. There was sufficient time left before the new season began to contact all her suppliers and inform them that she could no longer purchase their product. Sadly there were some angry scenes which Caitlin did her best to control but there were several occasions when she had to close the store to prevent damage or stealing. As a result of ceasing to trade in maple syrup, there was a considerable reduction in the number of people coming to the store.

Although the demand for whale oil had never been higher, at approximately the same time as the demise of the sugar trade, the focus of the whaling industry now moved down to the eastern seaboard of America primarily to the New England towns of Boston and Nantucket. With a considerable degree of peace now being enjoyed by this area, it made more commercial sense for the whaling fleet to land its precious cargo close to the most densely populated areas, rather than land their cargo at St John's and for the oil to complete it's journey in smaller coastal vessels.

The direct and unfortunate result of this departure of the whalers was that the barrel making enterprise which had been highly successful over the last ten years also declined. The cooperage did continue, though on a much smaller scale, as the cod fishing industry on the Grand Banks off the coast of Newfoundland continued to thrive and still needed barrels for the export of their salted catch and it's highly-prized cod liver oil.

Alone now, Caitlin tried desperately hard to keep her businesses profitable, often working far into the night long after the children were asleep. As a wealthy and still relatively young widow, she did not lack for offers of companionship and love. Some of these were probably sincere in their desire to help, console and to develop a genuine relationship, but there were also those who merely wanted control of her wealth, not only of her money, but also of the properties that she and David had bought throughout the town over the past few years, as well as acquiring their own house and the store. But she would have none of it, saying,

"David may no longer be here by my side, but my heart will never belong to anyone else."

Throughout these trying times, Callum Logan was a tower of strength to her. He had always taken his teaching duties seriously and soon became treated as one of the family. He would appear at her side just at the moment when she needed him; always ready to listen to her woes and to tender good advice when it was appropriate to do so, without trying to take over. But despite all the rumours and gossip that spread through the town that Caitlin wouldn't be a widow for very long and that Callum had only taken the position to gain control over her money, the relationship was purely platonic. They became great friends but as if by tacit and mutual agreement, Callum never tried to advance their relationship and Caitlin was happy to keep it that way.

Finally, the years of hard work caught up with her. She had been running and expanding the store, setting up the businesses of maple syrup production and managing the cooperage almost single-handedly; not to mention raising two small children and looking after her husband whose mental disabilities created far greater demands on her time and energy than if he had been physically injured or incapacitated. As a woman who had never been given to minor illnesses, colds or indeed anything that might get in the way of her working day and night for her businesses and family, it was not surprising that finally her lifestyle took its toll. Eventually, just over a year after David's death, she developed a wracking cough that made her gasp for breath.

Despite taking various medications and inhalations, probably because of her years of self-neglect, she contracted pneumonia and was confined to bed for several months. While she was sick,

Little Joe proved his worth and continued to run the store and the cooperage almost as well as she would have been able to herself. Although she was very ill, she would still try to involve herself in the activities of her businesses, until Callum and Little Joe, who were quite capable of running everything between them, paid her a visit together and told her in no uncertain terms that she should concentrate all her energies on recovery and leave the rest to them. It wasn't that she didn't trust her employees, but that she had been so used to doing everything herself that she found it almost impossible to let go.

During her illness, Caitlin had plenty of time to reflect on her life and to realise that with the commitments she already had in Newfoundland and her deteriorating health, she would never be able to return to Scotland. She knew that she had had several pieces of good luck that had come to her just at the right moment, but she was also aware that she had grasped her good fortune and used it to her own advantage. She had met some good people along the way who had helped her when she needed it most, but she had repaid them by being a good friend and neighbour to others when they in their turn had been in need. Even after all the years that had passed, she still recognised that the terrible deeds, the expulsion of the villagers and the murder of her relatives that she had witnessed in the glen should never be forgotten but that she herself had not been in a position to make the redress that the events so rightfully deserved. But now for her it was too late

So one evening, as her condition deteriorated, she called her daughter to her and said,

"Margaret Mary, I have something to tell you which you must remember for the rest of your life. You can do nothing about it now because as yet you are too young, but I hope and pray that one day you'll be able to do the things I vowed to achieve but haven't been able to. Listen carefully, for if you can't keep my promise either you too must pass it on to your own children. These things must never, ever be forgotten and I think your brother is too young to understand."

Caitlin began to tell her daughter the story of her life; of the way it was in the glen before the soldiers came, of how she and her family were driven from their home, and the adventures that she had had on her way to Canada and the subsequent events that led to their present situation. Her daughter listened quietly throughout the tale which took some considerable time due to the pauses the sick woman had to make whilst she recovered from each bout of coughing. When Caitlin had finished, Margaret Mary, her eyes wet with tears, went across to her mother, knelt beside the bed, laid her head in her lap and said quietly,

"The men who did these awful things to our family must be punished even if it takes a thousand years."

Caitlin's voice was for once clear and calm.

"You must not blame the actual men who came to the glen, Margaret Mary. They were only doing what they were told; either for money or, more likely because they were in fear of what might happen to them or their own families if they refused. No, the people who did us the greatest wrong were the faceless English lords whose only interest was profit and who didn't care whom they destroyed in the process. They knew only too well what the consequences of their actions would be but they chose to feign ignorance to keep a clear conscience. The abuse of power and the plundering of simple people, as we were in the glen, is truly wicked. Nobody has the right to destroy the lives and homes of others just for material gain. That is why over the years in our business I have tried to be fair with the local native people and include them in our dealings rather than exploit them. Which," she added. "would have been very easy to do."

Margaret Mary, seeing how tired and weak she was, stood up and took her mother's frail hand into hers.

"I promise to try to do as you ask Mother, but now you must rest. We will talk again tomorrow."

Margaret Mary never had the opportunity for that further talk with her mother because during that night Caitlin, exhausted by the mental and physical effort of relating her tale, slipped peacefully away to eternity, content in the knowledge that she had passed on to her offspring the promise she had made.

If David's funeral had gathered together almost the entire population of St John's, Caitlin's was more a gathering of all the peoples of Newfoundland. Groups came from all over the island. Some people travelled for several days on foot, canoe or by sailing boat along the coast. Native people from the many different tribes were represented as well as the whaling community, the fishermen, the dock workers and the loggers not to mention every shopkeeper and local dignitary for miles around. Her coffin, covered in the flowers of early spring, was born to the church on the shoulders of six smartly uniformed Marines from the garrison who had served under Lieutenant Blake when he was stationed in the port and who had known and loved Caitlin when she had lived amongst them in the garrison. Many of the townsfolk lined the route or clustered round the little church which was far too small for all the mourners to get inside. It was a moving sight to see the men in their tall black hats and women in their bonnets standing silent and motionless side by side with the local Indian men and women in the finery of their tribal costumes. Caitlin was laid to rest beside her husband in the little cemetery on the hillside above the harbour, far away from her relatives but surrounded by her family and the friends who loved her so well.

CHAPTER FIFTEEN

When she first became unwell, Caitlin, realizing that there were no immediate family members around to care for her children should she pass away, had made a will that included the provision for their education and wellbeing. Her dearest friend, Callum Logan, the children's tutor had agreed to become their guardian and with Callum, Little Joe and the bank as executors, their financial security was assured. She stipulated that, other than a generous allowance for her employees, all her money, which even after the decline of the business, was considerable, was to remain in trust under the guidance of the executors for her children until Charles reached the age of twenty one.

In the strange way that characteristics and abilities are handed down from generation to generation, Margaret Mary and Charles could not have been more different to either of their parents. Not so much in physical appearance but in their characters and attitudes. As they grew into adulthood, they developed personalities that could not have been more unlike those of their parents.

Margaret Mary had inherited her mother's beautiful red-gold hair, her fine figure and supple strength; whereas Charles was tall, slim and dark; much like his father had been as a young man. But this was where the similarities ended. Despite the fact that both of them had been brought up with the example of hard work by both parents and had been expected to help out at home or in the store from an early age, neither of them had any wish to follow in their footsteps. By the time she was fourteen years old, Margaret Mary was fully aware that her beauty, her undeniable charms and her comfortable financial circumstances made her a desirable catch for the young men of the town. She was vain and manipulative to the extent that she was quite happy to play one suitor off against another, and their parents too, if necessary, to achieve whatever it was she wanted.

Callum did his best to curb her headstrong ways, but she was spirited enough to point out that he was only her tutor and temporarily in charge of her finances, not her keeper and that she would make her own decisions as soon as she was old enough to be in control of her own money. When Little Joe tried to remonstrate with her, she simply told him that he was 'only an ignorant savage' and that she would never take any notice of any 'damn redskin.'

Charles, in contrast to his sister was neither arrogant nor headstrong. He was simply lazy and content to let others make decisions for him. He would complete the studies that his tutor had set for him, putting as little effort into them as was possible then disappear down to the waterfront where he could be seen loafing around with the other youngsters. It was inevitable that as he grew older he would begin to frequent the dockside taverns and ale houses and would return home late at night totally drunk and incoherent. Callum, as his guardian eventually refused to give him any further money with which to pursue his dissolute lifestyle but even this did not stop him, and when his debts began to get out of control, Charles was only too glad to agree to be enrolled at a law school in Boston Massachusetts if Callum would pay off from his inheritance all those to whom he owed money.

True to form, Charles continued with his self-indulgent lifestyle and passed his final exams with the lowest marks possible to allow him to qualify. He never showed the slightest interest in women and he never married. He seemed content enough to spend his days with his drunken and dissolute friends; so perhaps it was inevitable that he was stabbed and died in a bar-room brawl about a year after he had qualified. His estate, or what was left of it, reverted to his sister.

Where she got her high-handed and arrogant attitudes from, nobody knew, certainly not from her parents who had always been modest and had tried to raise their children to be good, upright citizens. There was little regret in St John's when Margaret Mary met a, young, rich and influential banker by the name of Thomas Alden from Philadelphia whose ship was storm-bound in the port for several weeks. Having made sure that his credentials were acceptable, she decided to use him as her way to escape from, what she described as 'the hell hole that is St John's'.

Once the decision had been made, she used her undeniable charms to attract his attention and soon convinced Thomas, whose father owned one of the largest banks in the city, that she was the girl that he had been looking for. Margaret Mary was invited to visit Thomas at his parent's house, ostensibly for a holiday but in reality to be vetted by the young banker's family to decide that she was a suitable young lady for a man of Thomas's standing to marry. Although she had never left Newfoundland before, Margaret Mary, by utilising her beauty, quick wit and a great deal of audacity, managed to gain the necessary approval. Once she was married and safely installed in Thomas's grand mansion in Philadelphia, by making the best use of her own looks, personality and independent means as well as her husband's banking friends and contacts she immediately became involved in the most snobbish circles of 'society'.

Complete snob that she was, Margaret Mary was slightly ashamed of her background as a storekeeper's daughter; so, desperate for approbation cut all ties with her home town and never returned to Newfoundland. She had never approved of Charles's dissolute ways and having left St John's, she never spoke to her brother again, indeed, she was unaware of his death until she was contacted by lawyers, some months after it had happened, regarding the distribution of his estate.

When Margaret Mary heard that her brother had been unmarried when he died and because she was his next of kin, his share of the business was now hers, she immediately wrote to Callum Logan and instructed him to sell all their assets in St John's and after paying off any debts Charles may have had, to send the remainder of his estate to her in Philadelphia.

Despite severing all connections with St John's, Margaret Mary did, as soon as they were old enough, pass on to her daughters the story and the promise that her mother had made. Over the next few generations, "Caitlin's promise", as it became known over the years, was assiduously passed down from mother to daughter but nothing was done to resolve it. In fact, the whole story of what happened that day in Glen Ceitlein would have vanished without trace had it not been for an amazing set of coincidences almost a hundred years later.

CHAPTER SIXTEEN

Shortly after the beginning of the twentieth century Caitlin's great great granddaughter Hannah married Travis Wainwright, a second lieutenant in the American army and within two years they had a daughter, Maria. Travis was a young man from an affluent family in Baltimore. He was a good, diligent soldier and his promotion, no doubt in part due to his family connections, was rapid. By the time he was sent to Europe to fight in the final battles of the First World War, he had risen to the rank of colonel. His active service was however tragically and ignominiously cut short when, almost as soon as he had reached the trenches of the front line, he contracted dysentery, was evacuated to a field hospital far from the enemy lines and died a few days later never having engaged in hostilities. The short time he spent in battle-torn Belgium had enormous influence on other members of his family many years later because; had he not perished in that distant land, his widow would never have travelled to Europe and thus never met her second husband.

Whilst Hannah was on a trip to Europe to visit her husband's grave less than a year after the armistice had been signed, she and her companion, also a widow, decided to visit France's capital and enjoy the delights of some of the famous attractions, including the Folies Bergere. During her stay in Paris she met and became involved with a man who claimed he was a Polish Count. His pedigree was probably dubious, most likely heavily embellished to secure access to the American woman's wealth. Whatever its authenticity, his assurances were successful because Hannah married him within a few weeks and moved to Poland, where she, and her money, disappeared leaving no trace. However, before she left Paris, where she had been staying with her new husband, Hannah wrote to her daughter Maria a letter explaining that she felt it was better for her to remain with her grandparents in America, at least for the time being until her mother was settled in Warsaw. Retrospectively, it was obvious that she had no intention of ever sending for her daughter because also in the letter she told her the story of 'Caitlin's Promise', thus neatly sidestepping any responsibility for trying to fulfil the obligation herself.

Upon its delivery in America, Maria's grandfather opened and read his daughter's letter to her child and rightly or wrongly decided that it was not the appropriate time to burden his granddaughter with additional responsibilities. He did not show the letter to her immediately but filed it away intending to reveal the contents when she was older and more mature, but this never happened, whether deliberately or simply because of the failing memory of an elderly man we shall never know. This letter was the last communication ever received from Hannah and Maria continued to live with her grandparents until she married in 1925.

She died at the ripe old age of ninety three, without ever knowing of her ancestor's desire.

As a consequence of this action, or rather inaction, 'Caitlin's Promise' lay concealed for the next two generations and only came to light again because of further remarkable coincidences.

When Maria's great granddaughter Emily Grooten was in her teens and living in Newark, New Jersey, she became interested in the origins of her family and began to produce a family tree to try to discover where her ancestors had come from. Her parents were able to supply the details for the first couple of generations, but beyond that point, though none of the generations seemed to have moved very far from the east coast of America, things became progressively harder and harder. To help in the search she would show her relatives, particularly the more elderly ones the diagram of what she had found out so far and ask them if they could fill in any of the gaps. She also requested permission to read through any old papers that they might have tucked away somewhere to glean such information that they might contain.

Most of these documents were of little help but she spent many long afternoons, when visiting her elderly aunts, uncles and cousins, sorting through dusty old boxes of faded photographs and stacks of useless correspondence that had been brought down from the attic for her to look at. Some of the information she found was of considerable interest as a fascinating insight into her family's past, but totally unrelated to her genealogical search. Undeterred, she persevered, until finally in the bottom drawer of a great uncle's desk, she was delighted to uncover the letter from Hannah to her daughter. There was no explanation as to how the letter had come to be in the desk and nobody that she talked to could shed any further light on the matter. They had been unaware of its existence although they had heard scandalous rumours that a member of the family had run off with a Polish Count.

In appearance, Emily was not dissimilar to how Caitlin had looked when she left the land of her birth and travelled to Newfoundland; fair hair, fine skin and an adolescent grace that promised great beauty in years to come. Her looks could have come from genes introduced from many other sources throughout the years of history, but, if she had been barefoot and wearing her plaid and shawl like the other young women she would not have looked out of place as an inhabitant in Glen Ceitlein at the time of the expulsion. However, it was in her character that the greatest similarity came to the fore. Her qualities of determination and reluctance to admit defeat were just the same as those of her ancestor. Of course there were enormous differences in their outlook, because Emily was an emancipated girl of the early twenty-first century, without any of the constraints, the ignorance and lack of education that were commonplace in Caitlin's time.

When Emily graduated from High School she was accepted by the university in Boston to study history. Knowing from the searches she had already made that her ancestors had originated from Scotland, she decided to take as the major project for her degree. "The Highland Clearances and the effects of Scottish Immigrants on the Development of New England." It seemed to her that this subject would link her Scottish origins with the American dynasty which had been created by Caitlin's monumental voyage to the New World. It had also occurred to her that she could combine her research with her own, long-term enquiries into her family's past whilst at the same time studying for her education.

There had not been too many difficulties tracing her lineage back to Caitlin in St John's, but there was very little information to be had, particularly in America, that was any great help to her to take her enquiries any further back across the Atlantic.

With the increasing need to research further afield for her studies and because she was getting more and more fascinated by her ancestors; when plans for a family holiday during her second summer were discussed, Emily persuaded her parents that it would be in the interests of furthering their daughter's education to take her on holiday to Scotland to visit the places where she might be able to discover Caitlin's birthplace and maybe even information on previous generations.

From Hannah's letter and a few other unconnected details that she had been able to glean from photographs and from conversations with her ageing relatives, Emily had been able to narrow down the area of search considerably. So even before she arrived in Scotland with her parents, she knew that they should concentrate their efforts on the district, south of Fort William but north of Inverary; which indeed was the area where Caitlin had been born and raised. Glen Etive actually joins the sea about five miles north of Oban, about halfway between these places.

In Scotland at the beginning of the nineteenth century, there was no legal obligation or requirement for any complete population census to be carried out, so it was only by scrutinising all sorts of local archives and in particular church records of births, marriages and deaths that Emily was able to discover from where Caitlin had actually originated. Once Caitlin's origins had been narrowed down to Glen Ceitlein, the trail became somewhat easier and one night sitting in her hotel room, Emily logged on to a website on the internet that helped you to trace your ancestry. Whilst browsing through the pages that were connected with Glen Ceitlein, she was astonished to find that someone else was searching for relatives from the very same place.

Making contact with the other searcher was relatively easy through the auspices of the website and as a result of the exchange of many emails that night, each was able to assist the other with information that would help them in their quest.

The man on the internet was a Mr Bruce Tulloch, who lived in Albany, New York State, not far from Emily's home town of Newark and had, for many years been seeking information about his family name. Sadly, he was suffering from a form of multiple sclerosis which meant, much to his disappointment, he would never be able to make the trip to Glen Ceitlein. He had put an enormous amount of effort into his search and although the family that he was seeking was not Emily's, it was however, one of the other two that had been living in the glen at the same time as Caitlin and had been subjected to the same eviction. To enable her to have a much more rounded picture of the little settlement of both their ancestors, he sent Emily a brief account of his own family during the first few years after having been driven from their homes, in the form of the following attachment to an e-mail:

"After having been driven from Glen Ceitlein in 1799, my family (the Tullochs) were forcibly relocated to a small patch of land with poor soil a few miles south of Oban, on a steep hillside overlooking the sea. The views were spectacular, but fine views do not fill the empty stomachs of a family, so to augment their income, the men of the family, father and three sons, took employment in the slate quarry on Easdale Island, the tiny island just beyond the Isle of Seil, only a few miles from their miserable home. Slate from Easdale was becoming a popular choice of roofing material and as the industrial revolution gathered momentum, demand grew with it. Large numbers of houses and tenements in Glasgow, throughout Scotland and even further afield were roofed in Easdale slate.

For the next hundred years or so the men of the Tulloch family worked in the slate quarry at Easdale, becoming extremely skilled workers, especially in the art of splitting the slates ready for the roofs of the homes and factories that were being built in huge numbers in the ever-growing towns and cities of Britain during the Industrial Revolution.

Most of the Easdale slate quarry is below sea level and only about a hundred yards from the seashore. In 1922 when production was at its peak, there was an unusually violent storm that happened to coincide with high spring tide, that flooded the entire workings irreversibly and in so doing destroyed a complete industry along with the livelihoods of several hundred people,

including all the members of the Tulloch family that were still
working there. With little alternative employment available at
that time, anywhere along the west coast of Scotland, most of
the Tulloch family emigrated to America, particularly to New
York where the construction industry was flourishing. There are
still many Tullochs in the New York telephone book though my
parents moved to Albany soon after the Second World War."

Having received this information and Bruce Tulloch's best wishes
for the success of her search, Emily replied, supplying all the information that she had obtained about her own family so far and
included everything else that she thought would be of any use to
him in his own search. She also promised him that once she had
visited the glen herself she would send him photographs that would
give him an actual picture of the site and the remains of his ances-
tral home. The only thing that Emily and Bruce had been able to
discover about the third family that had lived in Glen Ceitlein was
that one of them had been called Shinty McTain. It was not even
clear whether the name belonged to a man or a woman.

By now it was 4.00 am and although she was very weary, Emily
felt elated to have discovered so much background information that
seemed to make sense. But there was still no trace of any of the
other members of Caitlin's own family after they had been driven
from the glen. With her mind still racing, trying to assimilate all the
new information, she felt wide awake, but as soon as she climbed
into her bed, Emily, with the innate ability of the young adult, fell
fast asleep.

CHAPTER SEVENTEEN

When Emily and her parents arrived in the glen it was as cold and damp as only a Scottish day can be. Soft rain pattered on their waterproofs trying desperately to find its way through the slightest gap in their clothing. A light wind was making the bracken sway and the cotton grass nod gently. They left the car parked beside the tarmac road that still followed the original path of the old packhorse route, headed off down the steep track that led to the old bridge over the river and walked the two miles or so along the uneven, stony trail that led to the entrance of Glen Ceitlein.

They turned off the main track and soon came to the little valley where Caitlin's house had been. The rough trail soon became only a footpath that led them past some stone sheep pens which were obviously still being used. The iron gates and hurdles propped up against the mossy, stone walls were old and rusty and the grass in the pens had been trampled into mud by hundreds of sharp hooves, indicating recent usage. Having left the fanks, as sheep pens are called in this part of Scotland, behind, they continued for about another half mile, climbing steadily, until they came to the place where the houses had once stood.

Over two centuries had passed since these dwellings had been abandoned, but the rounded stones of the granite walls were still largely intact, though in places covered with moss. Of the windows and doors nothing was left. The roofs no longer existed of course, having been burned when the expulsions had occurred. Only the doorsteps, slightly dished and worn smooth by the passage of many feet gave any real indication that this place had been the permanent home of many generations of people. The little fields were now no more than a flatter part of the landscape, their boundaries marked only by straight grassy ridges across the hillside. Though the walls and the doorsteps were the only visible signs of the site ever having been inhabited, it wasn't difficult to imagine how it might have been; the low houses, the smell of peat smoke, the sound of voices, children playing. In fact all the things that would have made this place home to Caitlin's family and to her neighbours. The only big difference was that in Caitlin's time there would have been a lot more trees and scrub all around the area. All evidence of woodland would have been cleared by the charcoal makers in their quest for fuel for the furnaces of the Bonawe iron foundry. Any saplings that had tried to grow back would soon have been nibbled off to the ground by the ravenous sheep of the English landlords.

It was not a day to linger, or to wander round the empty site and let the mind drift back into the past, trying to conjure up visions of how the settlement might have looked when their ancestors were still in residence. By now Emily and her parents were thoroughly chilled and soaked to the skin. All they really wanted was to return to their hotel in Ballacullish and have a hot bath and a warm drink. But before they could indulge in these longed-for luxuries there was work to be done. The steady, unceasing rain made it impossible to sketch the outlines of the buildings and their relationship to each other, which would have enabled them to project, at a later date, how it might have looked when the rooms were still intact and houses inhabited. A few quick measurements were made and some photographs were taken, on cameras protected from the rain as best they could; some shots of the whole site and the views from the ruins, and others of the family standing beside the remains of the houses of their ancestors. Shots of the whole glen and surrounding mountain scenery were also taken to be sent back to Mr Tulloch in America. When they had done all they could, they stood for a few minutes in silence. But the weather soon brought them back to reality. It was time to leave.

Little was said on the long, dismal walk back to the car, their separate minds trying, in their own individual way to make sense of the 'maybe's', 'if only's' and 'what if's' that were going round and round in their heads.

Lee Grooten, Emily's father, was a big man, softly spoken and amenable almost to the point of being henpecked; but no one made any objection when he suggested that once they had returned to the hotel, warmed up and changed into some dry clothes, they should have some time for individual reflection before they met up again that evening for dinner. Even his wife Patricia, who was normally never short of an opinion, usually contrary to that of her husband, agreed that there were a few things that she needed to try to get clear in her head.

When once again she was warm and dry, Patricia left her husband resting comfortably on his bed, flat on his back with his hands clasped behind his head, staring into space. As she crossed the hallway, she peeped into her daughter's bedroom and saw that she was already typing away furiously on her laptop, totally oblivious to everything around her.

She didn't interrupt Emily but went downstairs to the resident's lounge, which was thankfully empty and sat down beside the roaring log fire and staring into the flames, let her thoughts wander through the actual happenings and the emotions of the visit they had made that morning.

They had all heard the story of 'Caitlin's Promise' from the letter that Emily had unearthed and in the comfortable modern world of present-day America, it was easy to think of the whole thing as just that; a story. But now having been to the actual place where it had all occurred, to the site of the very house in which Caitlin's father and grandmother had been murdered, it all became so very much more real; too real and as she sat before the flames she shuddered at the dreadful memory. How right Caitlin had been all those years ago when she said that these deeds should never be forgotten. Emily's research had already determined that she, Patricia, was directly descended from Caitlin, the genes of the people of Glen Ceitlein were in her own body. So it felt very strange to her as she sat before the flames, had the letter to Maria from her mother, Hannah, not been lost and the story of the massacre had continued to be told, mother to daughter, she would have had the story passed to her by her own mother and thus would have become the one with the responsibility to redress the wrongs as Caitlin had determined they should. Or if that had not been possible, she would have had to pass the message on to Emily. But as she pondered, the realisation came to her that even though they had only found out about the promise by chance, it still meant that she was now aware of her obligation; that she was the person who should try to, at the very least, make the modern world aware of the terrible things that had happened in this part of Scotland almost two hundred years ago.

As dinner progressed that evening so the talking began and although they had all had the same experiences that morning, their attitudes had taken quite diverse paths. Lee was all in favour of investigating the matter then letting the whole thing drop.

"After all," he said. "all these terrible things happened a very long time ago. Everybody that committed the actual deeds and the wicked English landlords are long-since dead. I think we should let bygones be bygones." Emily, full of youthful zeal wanted to start protests to bring the original atrocities to the attention of the media; though what good that would do was open to a good deal of conjecture. Her mother was more inclined to pursue the British government for compensation for all those who had been uprooted by the Highland Clearances. The conversation went round and round without reaching any sort of conclusion. There were moments when personalities and opinions clashed but no serious disagreement marred the evening. Positive and negative thoughts and ideas probably balanced each other out and so the evening drew to a close, with no conclusion reached.

Finally, Lee stood up, stretched wearily and asked his family,

"Tomorrow is our last full day in Scotland, what would you like to do?"

After a short pause, Emily's mother, Patricia replied,

"If everyone else is agreeable and the weather is better, which it is supposed to be, according to the weather forecast, I would like to go back to Glen Ceitlein for a final look and to leave some sort of memento as a memorial."

The others were happy with the idea and after a little more discussion, they all agreed with Patricia's suggestion as to what that memorial might be before heading off for bed. It did not take any of them very long to fall asleep after a busy and eventful day.

CHAPTER EIGHTEEN

The following morning, after a good night's sleep and having made a trip to Fort William for purchases, they returned to the cottages in Glen Ceitlein. In contrast to the day before, the sun shone and only a few fluffy white clouds dotted the sky. The burn running past the ruined cottages was in full spate from the previous day's rain, its peat stained water making a rushing sound as it tumbled over the boulders. Beautiful in a dark, sombre and very wet way as it had been the day before, the glen was much more appealing in the sunshine and they were glad to have been able to visit in different weather conditions. They were fully aware of the tragic circumstances that had ended the life of this settlement, but their spirits were lifted by the sunshine and they began to appreciate what a unique and splendid location this was.

With no risk of the paper being turned into pulp, the sketches were drawn and a new set of photographs taken. When all these activities had been completed, Emily went across to her rucksack which she had propped against the mossy wall of one of the houses and opening it, withdrew a large package. Having extracted the contents, she walked across to where her mother was waiting and together they bent down and beside the sunken doorstep of each of the three cottages, with the help of a garden trowel, bought especially for the purpose, they planted a little red rose bush.

"After all," her Mother had commented over breakfast. "We don't know which was Caitlin's house and which was the Tullochs or the other family, whoever and wherever they are. But they all suffered the same dreadful thing. So it is only right that they are all remembered in the exactly the same way."

The planting complete, they stood in silence for a while, each wrapped in their own thoughts until the quiet of the morning was disturbed by the sound of a quad bike approaching across the hillside.

The rider was the gamekeeper and ghillie for the estate that owned Glen Ceitlein and much of the surrounding area besides. It was his job to encourage the game birds, the deer on the mountain and the fish in the rivers to thrive and multiply. He would accompany the estate owner and his guests to make sure they were as successful as possible whenever they went out shooting, stalking or fishing. He loved this glen, his place of work and recreation and although it was privately owned, he was happy to share this wonderful environment with walkers and climbers, provided they respected the tranquillity and unspoiled beauty of this place that was his home. He would often stop and chat to the walkers, the climbers and the sightseers because these conversations helped him get a more complete picture of what went on in the glen. More than once, the seemingly innocuous remarks made by a friendly hill walker had led to the apprehension of thieves or poachers.

Angus McTaggart pulled alongside the three walkers and switched off his engine. 'Good Mornings' were exchanged and a general conversation ensued with Emily's father explaining why they were in the glen. When he finished by mentioning the planting of the rose bushes, they stepped aside to let Angus see the plants, each beside a doorway, and was met with complete silence. The gamekeeper reached into his pocket, pulled out his pipe and tobacco pouch, carefully filled it and when it was well alight and emitting large puffs of smoke, he spoke again in his soft highland accent.

"I cannot permit these plants to grow here. No matter how bonny they are."

"And why not?" Demanded Patricia, in her forthright way. She was not used to having her actions questioned.

Angus paused a moment, puffing on his pipe, then turning on the seat of his quad, gestured down the glen to the far slopes of Glen Etive.

"In June, the hillside over there is just a mass of pale pinkish purple flowers. They are the damned rhododendrons, escaped from someone's precious garden no doubt, and beautiful though they are for a couple of weeks of the year they are the scourge and plague of this glen and of many others hereabouts. They have taken over the greater part of the hillsides and where they grow nothing else can survive. They smother out all other plants and they give nothing back in food for the animals and birds. So I dare not take the chance of something similar happening again with your roses. It would only take a few seeds to be scattered by the birds and to take root for the same disastrous thing to start all over again."

Emily's mother, never short of an opinion and somewhat annoyed that her good deed seemed likely to be undone responded somewhat aggressively.

"I am not going to let you or anyone else dig up these little plants. They have been planted as a memorial to our ancestors, who were driven from their rightful homes here in this glen by the tyrannical English. Forebears of your employer no doubt. If these little roses flourish and spread, then so be it. They will be to the Highland Clearances what the poppies are to the fields of Flanders."

"That may well be so, but I'm afraid I will just be digging them up myself when you have left and gone back to America. This glen must not be put in danger of being swamped by another alien plant like the rhododendron."

"If that's the case, then it looks like I shall be in these parts for a long time to come."

Seeing that Patricia was not going to back down, Angus took refuge in his capacity as an employee. It was quite unusual for him to have his authority challenged in this way because, although he was technically nothing more than a full-time and trusted employee of the estate, in reality this was his own little kingdom where, in most matters of daily routine his word was law. Even the rich and famous who came to the estate for the shooting and fishing would accept without hesitation any decisions that he made.

"I will away to speak to my boss. I think he should be the one to sort this out."

The meek and mild Lee had not uttered a word during this exchange. He merely looked at the ground and kicked at a mossy stone with his boot and continued saying nothing. He had learnt over thirty years of marriage that the best policy was not to interfere with his wife when she refused to change her mind once she had decided on a course of action. She needed no encouragement when it came to argument or confrontation and he knew better than to suggest that she might be mistaken.

Emily, who had also been silent through all these altercations, took a step forward and made a diplomatic suggestion.

"What if I go with Mr. McTaggart and try to explain what's happening to his boss? How do you feel about that, Mother?"

"Not a bad idea at that" interrupted Angus quickly, seeing that this might be a way to escape from further argument and to pass all responsibility to someone else.

"If you must. Though I don't see how he will be able to help". grumbled her Mother, in no mood to climb down from her pedestal of righteousness. "Those little roses are gonna stay planted."

Patricia spread her un-needed waterproof coat on the grass and sat down carefully beside one of the little rose bushes with her back against the wall out of the wind; her body language indicating that she was settling in for a very long stay.

Emily perched herself somewhat precariously on the rear carrier of the quad bike and with her arms clutched tightly round the waist of the ghillie and her legs dangling precariously, they set off down the glen.

'Perhaps things are not all bad today.' thought Angus. It was a very long time since a pretty young girl had put her arms around his waist, so to make sure she had no opportunity to release her grip, he perhaps did not always select the smoothest parts of the track.

After a twenty minute ride, hair raising and uncomfortable for one and enjoyable for the other, they arrived safely at their destination without serious mishap.

Dalness House is the only really large house in the whole of the thirteen mile length of Glen Etive. It is the centre of the Glen Etive Estate which extends to about twelve thousand acres around the house and includes almost the whole of Glen Etive and much of the mountain and moorland that surrounds it. Constructed of pale grey stone giving it an air of permanence and grandeur, the house with its eleven bedrooms, stable blocks and coach houses, turrets and balconies was originally built in the late 1800's for use as a hunting lodge, and apart from a couple of cars parked outside, Emily could have been forgiven for thinking she had been transported back to the times when ladies wore long skirts and magnificent hats the men sported smart pointed beards.

As Angus and Emily drove into the stable yard, a young man in a dark green tweed jacket and jeans was walking across the cobbles from the offices in what had originally been the stables, towards the main house. As the quad bike came to a standstill in the shade of a large birch tree in the corner, Emily climbed stiffly from the hard and unforgiving carrier on the back, glad that the rough ride was over and she could relieve the aches and numbness in her behind.

The young man came across towards them and Angus introduced him as Richard Caudwell, the son of the owner. Probably in his mid-twenties, tall and broad shouldered with thick dark hair and clear brown eyes. As soon as he grasped her hand in a firm handshake and smiled in greeting, she was lost.

"If this is a poacher you've been out and caught Angus, then this is the prettiest one you've brought in yet." remarked Richard with a cheeky grin.

"It's no what she wants to take, it's what she wants to leave behind that's the trouble Sir."

"Perhaps you had better explain yourself, Angus," replied Richard.

This the ghillie did, trying his best to be tactful but at the same time absolutely adamant, that the rose bushes were potentially a serious threat to the well-being of the whole estate. Whilst still being polite, he made sure that Richard was well aware of the stubbornness of Emily's mother. Unaccustomed to needing ratification of his decisions, he finished rather lamely by saying,

"So I thought I had better come back and see what your father would want me to do."

Slightly annoyed that Angus had chosen to preclude him from the negotiations, electing to go over his head and to wait for his father to return and deal with the situation; in a somewhat more official tone, rather than the easy-going way he had spoken previously, Richard said to Angus,

"Thank you Angus, my father is not here today but I'm sure he would want me to try to resolve this matter myself. Please leave this with me and I will see to it that the young lady is reunited with her parents. I'm sure that I can persuade Emily and her parents to leave the glen peacefully and without removing any of your precious wild life."

At this obvious dismissal, with a brief nod of his head in acknowledgement, Angus tipped his deer stalker hat to Emily, started the engine on his quad and drove out of the stable yard towards the little cottage at the back of the big house. It was obvious from his body language, the stiffness of his receding back that he was very unhappy with the way that he had been excluded from any further part in the episode. Obviously he considered Richard to be just the son of his employer.

Richard turned to Emily and with a smile said,

"I was just on my way to the kitchen for a cup of tea; will you join me and let's see if we can work something out?"

"Sure, why not."

Richard led the way through a narrow passage, that led out of the stable yard and into a small paved courtyard at what was obviously the back of the main house. He opened the heavy studded kitchen door and stood aside for her to enter. As soon as she stepped across the threshold, Emily felt the years disappear; it seemed as if she had been taken straight back to the Victorian era; tall windows set high up on the walls, a huge black cooking range set into an alcove, cupboards lining the walls and an enormous, scrubbed pine table dominating the centre of the room. The high ceiling gave the room an airy feel. The only concessions to modernity were a gas cooker next to a white porcelain sink with shining stainless steel taps and an electric kettle on the dresser under the window. With those exceptions, the room could have been the film set for a television period drama.

Emily's mouth must have dropped opened, because, as Richard busied himself filling the kettle, he laughed and said.

"We don't live here all the time, you know. Most of the year we live in our house in London, with all mod cons. Dad deliberately left everything untouched here, just how it was when he bought it, except for paint and maintenance of course, because he thought that since it was so different from our other house, it would seem a little bit like an adventure every time we came. And I think he's right. The whole house is just the same. The only real change we've made is to install a new wood-fired central heating system and insulation wherever we could. It certainly needed it. Now it's nice and warm inside the house when we come up for Christmas and New Year, even though it's freezing and snowy outside."

"I think it's just great," replied Emily. Her eyes roamed the enormous room and she tried to imagine it full of staff and the bustle of cooks preparing a traditional Christmas dinner. But her eyes and thoughts kept coming back to the man who was just getting a carton of milk from a fridge that had been cleverly concealed behind one of the original cupboard doors.

"Try that."

When Richard handed her a mug of hot tea, she realised just how thirsty she was. She leaned against the marble drainer beside the sink and holding the mug in both hands with the handle pointing away from her she was able to observe him better without him realizing what she was doing or seeming to stare. The more she looked, the more she liked what she saw.

For a minute or two, they stood in silence sipping their tea. The ticking of a big, old clock high up on the wall the only sound. Finally Richard, who had propped himself up on the rail in front of the ancient cooker, broke the surprisingly companionable silence.

She sipped her tea as he spoke.

"From what Angus said just now, it seems we have a bit of a Mexican stand-off. But I've only heard the story from his point of view. It was good of you to come all the way down here. It can't have been very comfortable for you on that quad. The carrier is more suited to carrying a stag or a chainsaw."

"It wasn't," Emily replied with a rueful smile. "I'm just beginning to get some feeling back in my behind now."

"Right. To business. What do you think Emily? Do you think there is an amicable solution to the problem? I know you seem to have become something of an involuntary mediator, but you must surely have an opinion?"

"What Angus says about the roses being alien invaders does make a lot of sense. I don't think it would have even occurred to my mother when she bought and planted those little bushes. It certainly didn't to me. I suppose we just assumed that the glen had always looked the way it does now with all the rhododendrons. The trouble is, when my mother decides to do something and then she's told she can't do it, she's inclined to dig in her heels. And when she does that, nothing short of a nuclear occurrence will make her change her mind."

Richard did not reply for a moment. He stood up, walked over to the sink and rinsed his mug.

"Then nuclear it shall be. When you've finished your tea, shall we go back to your parents and see what can be resolved?"

They chatted for a few more minutes whilst Emily gave Richard some more details of her quest for her ancestry and her long-standing interest in Glen Ceitlein and in return, Richard told her a little about his work as an aeronautical designer in London. Neither of them seemed in too much of a hurry to leave but finally, when she had drained her mug, Richard led her outside to a battered but serviceable green Land Rover.

CHAPTER NINETEEN

As they drove back down the glen, Richards's brain was working overtime, trying to come up with a solution that would enable the rose bushes to be removed and yet allow Patricia to leave the glen with her dignity intact. Even though they had just met and he really didn't know much about her, he was already greatly attracted to Emily and to antagonise her mother at their first meeting would hardly make for an auspicious beginning to any relationship with her daughter.

Compromise seemed the answer, but he had no idea how it could be achieved until just before they reached the half-way point of their journey. When they left the tarmac road, Emily jumped out and opened the gate to the track that led down to the river; too rough for a hire car, but easy enough for a Land Rover if you didn't mind a bumpy ride. As they were crossing the wooden bridge over the busy river that tumbled down Glen Etive, he saw below him on a small patch of open grass beside the water, a single large Scots pine tree seemingly standing as a sentinel over all who would use the little meadow. An idea began to form in his mind as to how to break the impasse.

Reaching the end of the stony road, at the point where the glens meet, Richard and Emily set off to walk the last, stony mile to the site of the settlement. Even Land Rovers cannot pass into Glen Ceitlein.

As soon as they arrived at the site of the cottages where Lee and Patricia were waiting, Emily introduced Richard to her parents upon whom he used his undeniable charm to try to persuade Patricia that it was expedient to allow the rose bushes to be removed. He explained that it could be detrimental to the entire ecology of the glen to introduce another alien species; even as innocuous as three simple little red roses might appear. His request was politely but emphatically refused.

"My ancestors lived here, my ancestors died here and some were even murdered here. Nobody has done anything to acknowledge their existence. Until today that is. And now you want to destroy the first act of recognition of their humiliating and murderous expulsion that these people have received in nearly two hundred years."

Richard was silent for a couple of minutes, as if deep in thought, but actually diplomatically waiting for the anger of the moment to diminish. Then speaking quietly he made a suggestion.

"My grandfather bought this estate about forty years ago with money earned by his family in the shipping trade, mainly on the Indian and Far-Eastern routes. So my family were not responsible in any way for the evictions from the glen. I didn't even know that anybody had ever lived in Glen Ceitlein. It had never occurred to me. I knew that these stone walls were here but I simply assumed that they were just more abandoned fanks. However, now that I do know of their existence and especially now that you have told me about the way that the people who lived here were forced to leave, I think it is right there should be a memorial to them, but perhaps one that is more in keeping with the glen itself."

Richard was silent for a while; partly to allow Patricia a little time to realise that he was prepared to agree with her proposal in some way, but also to add a little drama to the moment.

"So I propose that instead of the roses, we should plant three Scots pines that would grow to become great trees. They are an

160

indigenous species that grow well here and would serve as a permanent reminder to symbolise the way that the three families have flourished. There would be a fence around them to protect them from deer and this barrier would also let other native species naturally spring up around them. Perhaps there could be a small cairn with an inscribed stone built in to explain why the memorial is here. And if you like," he concluded in a final effort to placate Patricia, "We could make some mention of your name as the person who proposed this memorial."

"And what about the roses?" Patricia asked; still in a belligerent mood, remaining seated on the grass beside the little bushes. She didn't seem to have moved from the spot since Emily had left on that alarming journey seated on the back of the gamekeeper's quad bike.

"As Angus said, we can't take the risk of another rhododendron fiasco, but they could stay as a sort of guarantee until we have completed the memorial. Just for this season, we could let them flower but remove the rosehips before they release their seeds. That would encourage us to get a move on. Of course, the estate would pay for all this. I would have to get approval from my father who has the final say in matters like this. But I'm sure that he will agree and it will all be OK."

"What do you think, Lee?"

Patricia asked, looking up at her husband who was standing slightly to one side, apparently gazing at the magnificent view but actually listening intently to all that was being said.

Lee was a man of few words, he tried wherever possible to avoid any sort of confrontation; he usually found it less stressful just to agree with his wife but on this occasion and much to her surprise, he voiced an opinion that could be challenged.

"Sounds like a great idea to me. It would be a much more permanent thing. Scots pine trees live for ages, so any trees we planted could be here for hundreds of years. Long after we've gone. No problem with the contamination either, there are hundreds here already. And," he concluded, "they will certainly fit in well with the landscape. I also think that the cairn should be made from stones gathered from here in Glen Ceitlein, not the usual white stuff that they usually use to make memorials."

There was a long minute's silence, Lee, wondering a little nervously, if he had said the right thing; Patricia trying to decide if she could agree to her husband's suggestion without seeming to surrender too easily and Emily surprised that her mother had actually asked her father for an opinion at all and absolutely astounded that her father had been so forthright with his opinion.

"I suppose you're right." concluded Patricia reluctantly. "It seems strange to make such a fuss over three little rose bushes." She sighed dramatically. "But I suppose we have to be eco-friendly these days."

"It was probably only one or two rhododendron bushes that escaped, and look what havoc they caused. Here on the estate we are always trying to keep them in check, but it's a major task. I don't suppose we will ever eradicate them completely, but we won't give up the struggle," Richard replied.

Relieved that an agreement had finally been reached without serious argument or offence to anyone, Richard Caudwell invited Emily and her parents back to Dalness, ostensibly to iron out some details, so that when he spoke to his father, as he would be doing that night, there would be no problems with the proposal for the memorial. The invitation had the added advantage that it would also prolong the time he could spend with Emily.

When they all arrived back at Dalness, having stopped the Land Rover at the main road so that Lee could collect his car and follow them to the house, Richard's first action had been to seek out Angus McTaggart, and tell him the good news that a solution had been found to the impasse. The ghillie was highly gratified that his opinion had been upheld and although he had not been born in the glen himself, he agreed the memorial was entirely appropriate. His wife, who was the housekeeper at Dalness House, soon provided Richard and his guests with tea and oatcakes, apologising, with typical highland generosity, that had she known they were coming she would have been able to provide them with something more substantial.

Whilst they ate, they chatted amicably about the proposed memorial and how it might look when it had been completed. During the conversation, Richard asked Emily if she would like to help him draw up the necessary construction plans commenting that most of this could be done by email or telephone.

"How different communications are now compared to Caitlin's time." he commented.

When he suggested that she might also like to compose the inscription for the memorial tablet that was to be built into the cairn, Emily agreed almost too quickly, looked at Richard and blushed.

Tea and oatcakes consumed, names and contact details exchanged, Richard accompanied his unexpected guests back to their vehicle and as they were getting into the car to return to their hotel, Richard discreetly slipped a piece of paper on which he had written his private phone number into Emily's hand and said quietly so that nobody else could hear.

"Give me a call sometime".

She called him later that night, after she had left her parents and had gone to her own room and again the following morning from the airport while they waited for their flight back to America.

These were the first of many calls, texts and emails between the two of them that autumn, some it is true, concerning the design and progress of the monument project, but as time went on the conversations became more intimate and personal until in December, Emily was invited to Dalness to share in the Caudwell family celebrations for Christmas and New Year. With her dissertation almost complete and her studies for her final exams well ahead of schedule, Lee and Patricia agreed without hesitation, glad that their daughter had chosen to go back to Scotland rather than to indulge in some of the dubious, political student activities that were going on in Boston at that time and happy for her that she seemed to have fallen for someone who appeared eminently suitable.

Richard was at the airport on Christmas Eve to greet the girl whom he had only met for a few brief hours but who had already stolen his heart. He stood waiting at the arrivals barrier with his pulse racing, feeling equal measures of apprehension and excitement, little realising that Emily, collecting her suitcases from the carousel was having much the same feelings of trepidation as he was.

Their greeting was warm and friendly and having stowed Emily's cases in the boot of the car they set off through the maelstrom of traffic, inevitable on a Christmas Eve afternoon.

Leaving the congestion behind and passing through the outskirts of Dunbarton, the last town of any size on their route home, Richard swung the car off the road and into a service area that was ablaze with lights. There were Christmas decorations everywhere and they could hear sentimental carols coming from tinny-sounding loudspeakers up in the roof above the petrol pumps.

"This is the last twenty-four hour filling station we shall pass," Richard explained. "I always try to get home with as much diesel in the tank as I can. You never know when you will get another chance to fill up. Let's have a coffee before we get back on our way."

Refuelling completed, they headed towards the cafeteria and as they walked, Richard told Emily that a few years before Dalness had been completely cut off from the outside world for three weeks by several inches of snow that had been whipped up into a blizzard, the great drifts leaving all the roads totally impassable.

Emily instinctively clasped Richard's arm and looking up into his face whispered almost to herself.

"Please God that the same thing shall happen again this year."

There, in the shadow of a tired looking Christmas tree, and observed only by a large and rather tatty plastic Father Christmas, a platonic relationship of emails and phone calls dissolved into the wonderful reality of embraces and kisses for a young couple who were utterly oblivious to the comings and goings of the rest of humanity which was passing just a few feet from where they stood.

Darkness had fallen and the temperature was well below freezing by the time they began the descent from Rannoch Moor down into Glen Etive. The white frost sparkled on the trees and heather as the car headlights swung across the hillside as they turned and twisted down the narrow road; the whole world twinkling as if a million tiny lights had been switched on to greet their American guest. As they turned into the stable yard, Richard's parents Francis and Hazel, having seen the approaching lights, were standing beside the archway to give them a friendly welcome.

Dalness House was, as Richard had predicted back in the summer, warm and welcoming. The decision not to modernise the property in no way detracted from its comfort. Hot water, thick carpets and a wonderful, cosy bed greeted the weary girl when she finally left the friendly gathering downstairs; tired from her long journey, but blissfully happy.

The Christmas day that followed passed in a blur of burgeoning love, new but friendly people to get to know and the delightful problem of trying to find reasons for Richard and Emily to be alone for a few minutes. It was very obvious to the rest of the household and guests that romance had suddenly blossomed between the two of them, but everybody was delighted and too polite to intrude upon the magic of their moment.

On Boxing Day, the couple walked alone into Glen Ceitlein, where Emily was able to see the progress that had been made on the memorial. A small site on the hillside above the remains of the cottages had been levelled and along the rear edge had been planted the three Scots pine trees; quite small as yet with their short, flexible branches bent low by layers of thick hoar frost. The base for the cairn had already been laid, with many more freshly cleaned pieces of granite, gathered from higher up the hillside and from the bed of the stream, stacked nearby ready to complete the monument. It had been positioned so that a visitor could stand beside the cairn and look out over where the settlement had been with the three trees of remembrance standing in the background as living guardians.

Inspection of the memorial site completed to the satisfaction of them both, they turned to leave and as they passed the doorway of one of the dwellings, Emily stooped, cleared the frost from one of the rose bushes and in a gesture of goodwill, pulled it from the soil and handed it to Richard.

"The hostages can now be released." she said with a smile. "But do you think they could be planted somewhere else where they won't do any harm? I think they deserve to live."

"How about we retire them to the garden of our house in London? That'll be a much more appropriate place for them now."

It was inevitable that the solution to yet another problem was completed with another passionate embrace. Kissing seemed to be an excellent way to begin and end every action, discussion or description, or anything else that occurred on that blissful and precious day.

As they drove back up Glen Etive towards Dalness, the lights in the house were twinkling in the early twilight, bright with the promise of warmth and security for their return. A look passed between them that had no meaning but meant everything.

The rest of the festive season passed in a delicious romantic blur; new places, new people, new experiences intertwined with, best of all, a new love. For a few headlong days, nothing else mattered.

Hogmanay, the Scottish New Year was celebrated by the whole family in traditional style with pipers and great feasting. The haggis was duly acclaimed with great aplomb, and many toasts were proposed to the chinking of whisky glasses. Auld Lang Syne was sung and midnight was welcomed with Goodwill to all Men, with Richard and Emily's first public kiss being greeted with great approval by all those present.

They woke the following morning to a fairy-tale world of a deep blue sky, still tinged with the pink of the dawn and two inches of white, white snow. Gone were the greys, greens and browns of the day before, hidden beneath the most beautiful winter blanket. It was a day to enjoy Glen Etive in a different guise. There was no wind and not a cloud to be seen though the shadows were long as the low mid-winter sun only just managed to clear the mountain tops. As they walked beside the tumbling River Etive, the snow crunched under foot; snow that was undisturbed by any snow plough or human footprint. It was the softest, purest and most beautiful whiteness that Emily thought she had ever seen.

Suddenly, Richard stopped and took Emily's arm.

"Listen."

They stood in silence for a few moments.

"I can't hear anything."

Richard laughed softly.

"Exactly. One of the most precious gifts Glen Etive has to give us in our modern, noisy world. Silence."

Emily said nothing, but leaned slightly back against Richard's chest, her eyes closed, her cheeks pink from the frosty air. He folded his arms around her and they stood in silence for a while absorbed in each other and in the wondrous soundless surroundings.

Cold feet reminded them that it was not the sort of day to stand still for very long, so having decided that they had already walked up an enormous appetite, they retraced their steps to the house where a roaring fire was waiting to welcome them.

The beautiful white blanket of snow was soon gone however, which was just as well because it was all too soon time for Emily to leave Scotland and return to her studies and final examinations in Boston. Richard too had to return to his job in London where a completely new project, designing vital new components for a prototype short-haul passenger aeroplane awaited him.

Their parting at Glasgow Airport was reluctant and tearful but plans were already being made for a reunion in a few months' time.

CHAPTER TWENTY

Even though both of them had plenty of activities to fully occupy their lives, time was always found for the numerous, essential phone calls and emails that modern romance demands. Emily successfully graduated from university in June, with her major project and dissertation about the effect of the Highland Clearances on New England receiving considerable praise from her tutors and assessors. In late summer, when there was a convenient lull in his work, Richard travelled to America to visit Emily and her family. Of course, her parents had already met Richard in the glen and they warmly welcomed him into their home with typical New England hospitality.

As soon as they could escape from the seemingly endless round of family visitations, the couple took a few days off to drive through the beautiful countryside and caught the ferry across to Newfoundland to visit the little grave in St John's of Emily's ancestor Caitlin. As they stood arm-in arm in front of the lichen-covered headstone, they took a little time to remember the young girl who had been instrumental in bringing their pathways together. The two-hundred year gap had truly been bridged.

On a warm starry night at the top of Signal Hill overlooking the harbour, Richard went down on one knee and asked Emily to be his wife. A request she unhesitatingly accepted.

As is often the case with newly engaged couples, the whole of the following year was taken up with planning and consultation, arrangements and compromises; made all the more complicated by the oceanic division that was the inevitable result of Richard's work in London and Emily's family in Newark, New Jersey. They soon lost count of the number of texts, calls and emails that winged their way across the Atlantic, but the phone bills were substantial to say the least!

At the heart of all discussions was the desire to set up their marital home in Dalness House and all the arrangements that they made were with this in mind. To make it possible for Richard to work from remotest Scotland it required a good deal of technological wizardry to enable satellite communication to be installed in the house because down in a deep glen and far away from radio masts, ordinary phone signals were at best patchy and in most cases unobtainable. Even with the latest electronics, he would have to travel to London at least twice a month, but it was the best he could manage for the time being and still keep his job.

Emily was fearful that there would be nothing constructive for her to do at Dalness, but it was Angus McTaggart, the ghillie who sowed the seeds that resulted in the direction of Emily's plans for the development of the whole house. Maybe the perilous ride on the quad bike had helped eliminate any rancour, but they soon seemed like old friends. When she had been in Scotland over Christmas she had enjoyed several long conversations with him in which they had chatted about all manner of things, especially about his work and what it was like living in such a remote place. On one occasion, when Emily remarked about the glen's peacefulness and its loneliness, Angus had made the comment.

"What this beautiful place has in abundance is solitude, but what it needs is people; but it's awfu' hard to have both at that same time without ruining it completely."

This innocent remark ignited an idea in Emily's mind and after a great deal of talking it was decided that she would take an intensive course in Estate Management in New York before the wedding with a view to becoming involved in the running of the estate in Glen Etive. The long-term plan being to turn Dalness House into a haven of tranquillity where a very small number of paying guests would come and live with the family but have plenty of time to rest and refresh themselves in a beautiful secret place, away from the pressures of "society".

Both families became amicably involved in the wedding preparations, which required considerable effort because of the peculiarities of the long-distance organisation and the remote location where the ceremony was to take place.

In an extravagantly romantic gesture, Richard was waiting for his fiancée in the departure lounge of JFK Airport in New York to escort her back to his native country. This meant that he would have to cross the ocean twice in less than twenty-four hours.

Three days later, two years to the day after their first meeting, Richard and Emily were married at the little church in Taynuilt, further down Loch Etive, the nearest place of worship to Dalness, with many friends and relatives from both sides of the Atlantic sharing in the celebration. Much to his regret, Mr Tulloch, whose family had been neighbours of Caitlin Munroe in Glen Ceitlein was too ill to make the journey to Scotland, but sent them a message of goodwill and was represented at the wedding by his son and daughter-in-law.

After the ceremony, a flotilla of gaily decorated boats, large and small ferried the couple and their guests up to the head of the loch where a fleet of all-terrain vehicles was waiting to take the whole party as far as possible towards Glen Ceitlein. There on the hillside just above the ruined cottages, under an intensely blue and cloudless sky, the bride, radiant in a beautiful wedding dress and sturdy walking boots unveiled the plaque on the completed memorial to her ancestors. Just above the cairn, the three little Scots pine trees were already growing happily as testimony to those who had lived in this remarkable place in ages past.

In a fitting memory to Caitlin, included in the wedding feast were sweet dishes with plenty of maple syrup in memory of the frightened girl who made a success of her life and had begun the dynasty that was returning to its roots.

And so it is just twelve months later, that the little boy who sleeps in his cradle beside Emily, as she gazes from the window of Dalness House will inherit, in his time, among the many thousands of acres of the Glen Etive estate, the land in Glen Ceitlin that was brutally taken from his forefathers so many years ago.

Afterthought.

So, maybe, just maybe, the voice that I heard as I sat beside the waterfall, was Caitlin, chattering to her friends as they climbed to the cave high on the mountainside, before the soldiers came.

9 781783 240500